THE BLOOD RED SANDS OF MARS

MURDER ON MARS

By Greg Fowlkes

Includes an introductory story from the latest book
THE LAWS OF MAGIC

And introducing THE FICTIONAL DETECTIVE,
A Fictional Press Novel.

THE BLOOD RED SANDS OF MARS
MURDER ON MARS

© 2011 The Fictional Press
www.TheFictionalPress.com

Published by The Fictional Press

The Fictional Press, an imprint of Intrepid Ink, LLC, provides full publishing services to authors of fiction and non-fiction books, eBooks and websites. From editing to formatting, to publishing, to marketing, Intrepid Ink gets your creative works into the hands of the people who want to read them.

Find out more at www.thefictionalpress.com.

ISBN 13: 978-1-937022-12-9

Printed in the United States of America

Foreword

Mars has always held a fascination for science-fiction writers from Edgar Rice Burroughs' Barsoom novels to the present day. I admit to being no different. At the time *The Blood Red Sands of Mars* was written, Mars had morphed from a planet of canals built by an ancient civilization to something closer to reality due to the Mariner probes and the two Viking landers. This is the Mars that I chose to write about—a lifeless Mars where humans are confined to pressurized habitats and surface suits as they try to hack out a self-sustaining colony.

I also chose to make the novel a detective story. In part, this can be blamed on watching too much TV and too many Humphrey Bogart movies in my impressionable youth. The fact is I have always had a tendency to blend the genres. The first science fiction novel I tried to write (it was quickly aborted somewhere in chapter 2) was about a professor of detective literature in some distant future where crime had been eliminated who is called upon to solve the first murder that had occurred in a hundred years solely because he was the only one who had any idea of how to go about it. It wasn't a bad idea, I just wasn't ready to execute it. The four stories that make up my second published book, *The Laws of Magic*, are also mysteries of a sort. It is inevitable that once man starts living on other planets there will be crimes, thus the need for someone to solve them. That, at least, is the premise of *The Blood Red Sands of Mars*. As a mystery, it owes more to Raymond Chandler than to Agatha Christie, with apologies to both.

The title, *The Blood Red Sands of Mars*, strikes me today as a trifle lurid, but it seemed a good idea at the time. If I were to write the book today I would probably choose the more prosaic *Murder on Mars*, but I have decided to stick with the original title on advice of my publisher.

I wrote *The Blood Red Sands of Mars* in the late 70's. The version as published here was completed in January of 1979. As such, it reflects the naming conventions then in use, which were based on the results of the two Viking missions. Similarly, the details of the surface conditions and features are my imaginings based on information available at the time in magazines such as Scientific American and Astronomy. I have purposely not gone back and revised the story based on more recent data. I ask the reader to accept The Blood Red Sands of Mars for what it is, a thirty year old novel, written in the flush of youth.

Greg Fowlkes
Author
The Fictional Press
www.TheFictionalPress.com

1

The wind was blowing again against the west wall of the hut. He could hear the grains of sand abrading the thin aluminum skin that protected him from the outside. Through the window, half frosted from the continuous onslaught of sand and dust, he could see clouds of dust obscuring the sky. The sky was a pastel pink, a color no sky had any right to be. The wind, despite its 120 kph. velocity, made only a thin howl as it blew over the half buried cylinder of the hut.

McKernan lay on his cot trying not to admit that he was awake. It was a losing battle. After a few minutes he surrendered and glanced over at the clock sitting on the crate next to his bed. The dim red digits of the LED display read 7:58. It was too early to get up, too late to go back to sleep. He rolled over, shivering at the cold. The temperature couldn't have been more than ten degrees Celsius inside the hut. For the twentieth time he thought to himself that he would have to fix the heater before winter— if he could get the parts. Either that, or put in more insulation—if he could find that. The cold finally forced the decision to get up.

Standing, he felt the cold plastic floor beneath his bare feet. With his foot he fished the worn and patched pants from beneath the cot and pulled them on. He dug underneath his pillow and came up with a switchblade knife that he stuck in his pocket before drawing on the turtleneck sweater that had lain next to his pants. The cold feel of the cloth did nothing to dispel the cold from his body. From the crate he picked up a shoulder holster with a small automatic pistol and put it on. McKernan drew the weapon, worked the slide once, and after examining it perfunctorily, placed it back in the holster. Satisfied, he pulled on a worn pair of leather boots and placed another knife in a sheathe between his skin and the boot top.

Dressed, he went over to the shelf that served as counter and table. He put a pan of beans onto the heating unit and got a soysteak from the small refrigerator that held up one end of the shelf. The steak went into the frying pan on the other heating element. An egg would have been nice, but at the current price of three dollars apiece it was an extravagance that he would have to put off for a while.

As the food cooked he drew a liter of water from the spigot in the corner of the hut and watered the plants in the garden under the window. The carrots and tomatoes were doing nicely. He smiled briefly because it would be good to have fresh vegetables for a change. The big, leafy oxygen plants were doing well, too. He would be able to cut down on his oxygen ration this month and save some money.

He took the beans off the heating element and replaced them with the coffee pot. The beans were still half cold, but he wasn't in the mood to hassle with them. He only had the two heating elements, and he didn't want to have to wait for his coffee. He forced down the beans and then wolfed down the steak. It almost tasted like real beef, but then maybe his memories were fading. As usual, the coffee tasted terrible and tepid, too. The air pressure in the hut was too low for water to boil properly.

He finished his meal and scraped the remnants of food into the pressure vessel that served as a compost heap. The gauge on its neighbor showed that he had almost half a tank of methane. He'd be able to sell that soon and use the money for something useful, like a still. Completing his rounds, the gauges on the life support systems showed that everything was still working at keeping him alive. He went back to the pots and scrubbed them clean with sand. That, at least, was plentiful and cheap.

He checked his watch against the clock. It was time to get going. Pulling on his jacket he went to the airlock at the corridor end of the hut. After checking the gauge to make sure that there was pressure on the other side, he undogged the latches and stepped through. Closing the door behind him, he repeated the process with the outer hatch, latching both doors behind him. The outer door he locked with a heavy padlock.

He had entered a low tubular corridor made of the same aluminum foil and plastic foam construction as the hut. The walls, however, were even thinner, and no pretense was made of heating it. He could see his breath condensing in front of him as he began to walk down its length. It was a hell of a way to live, he reflected, not for the first time. But then, it had been hell living in L.A. where he'd been born, with brown air, rats, a chronic shortage of water, and overcrowded tenements. He had made his choice, but sometimes it seemed as though life was a continual shiver.

The corridor was pierced at regular intervals by hatches identical to his own. The huts behind the hatches were identical, too, except for the modifications the owners had made to make them more livable. This part of the city was old, dating back a couple of decades to the first days of the settlement when it had been part of a scientific base. The scientists had departed, at least from that corridor, and been replaced by those who had the money to buy or rent the huts from the Trust Authority. Maintenance was pretty much left up to the residents.

Along the sides and overhead ran the pipes and conduits that pumped in the gases, liquids, and power necessary for sustaining life. The whole system looked as jury rigged and fragile as it actually was, though surprisingly few people died whenever the system failed. Martians were a cautious lot. One didn't talk much about injuries. Accidents on Mars didn't leave many.

A hundred meters down the tube he came to an airlock. Going through the same ritual that he had used on his front door, he went through to another length of corridor indistinguishable from the one he had just left. Continuing on, he passed through two more airlocks until he entered a corridor that sloped downward. The hatches were farther apart, and larger. Signs overhead indicated the businesses or functions that were carried out behind them. The air was warmer because the corridor was buried beneath the sand which provided insulation. At the end of the tunnel was a larger airlock set into a wall of fused silica bricks, the first substantial piece of construction he had met that morning.

Passing through the portal was like entering another world, which in a way he had. This was the public Mars, the planet seen by the corporation men and the officials of the Trust Authority. It was also the planet seen by tourists, the brave new colony, man's first outpost on another planet. The tourists didn't really care to see the hut town. They were part of the same world as the corporation men and the government types. It still took a great deal of money or power to reach Mars.

The difference was more than one of degree. For one thing, the temperature was a comfortable twenty. For another, the walls were flat and met the floors and ceilings at right angles, unlike the inflated skins of the huts and corridors. With a little imagination it could almost be an enclosed shopping mall on earth, though the presence of fused silica blocks was more prevalent than any architect would allow.

The most important difference, however, was the sight of people scurrying along. He hadn't met anyone in the outer corridors. People rarely lingered there because of the cold. Now, McKernan could see at least twenty people and it was still fairly early. No airlocks interrupted this corridor. Extending for two hundred meters in either direction, it was twenty meters wide and ten high, the largest enclosed volume on the planet. Arrayed along its length were the offices and store fronts of the corporations that owned Mars, as well as the more prosperous saloons and bordellos.

One day the Trust Authority promised that the whole city would be like that, with apartments and condominiums for the ordinary workers, but neither the Authority or the corporations had yet come up with the money. For the moment all that existed was the one street of a few blocks.

McKernan headed towards the Authority's offices which dominated one end of the mall, but turned aside at the last moment when he noticed that a small, dark doorway was open. He knew that he should resist the temptation, but he was not in a very disciplined mood. He went through the doorway into the darkness beyond.

Finnegan's was the only real, honest bar on Mars. There were any number of saloons and even a cocktail lounge in the Mars Sheraton, but only one quiet, dark place where a man could drink in peace. McKernan felt the need for some of that peace at the moment.

He sat down on one of the stools before the only mahogany bar on Mars. Finnegan, himself, was behind the bar, though in fact he almost always was, no matter what the hour.   The bartender looked up and greeted the newcomer, "Good morning, constable. Beer or whiskey?"

"It's too early for beer. It's too early for whiskey, but give me a shot, anyway."

Finnegan poured out a shot glass of amber liquid and placed it before McKernan and then stood back polishing a glass while he studied the man opposite him.

McKernan knocked back half the glass before he spoke. When he did, there was a bitter edge to his voice. "Sometimes I wonder if it's worth it, Finnegan. I could be back on a planet fit for human life."

"Could you, now, constable?" Finnegan said, putting down the glass and picking up another in equally gleaming condition. "If mother earth was such a bed of roses, why are you here?"

He breathed on the glass and examined it against the light for a moment, then looked at McKernan with the same intentness. "You're here because you're not the sort to live off the dole or to spend your life with another man being your boss. Instead you'll spend your life trying to make this planet a fit place to live and retire in twenty years with a nice pension. Now drink up and get to work, laddy."

"Yeah, sure. Sorry to burden you with my problems. Early morning depression, I guess. See you." He finished off the shot and left five dollars in Authority script on the bar.

The bite of the whiskey so early in the morning didn't really help his disposition, but it did give him enough courage to make it to the office. The morning ritual at

Finnegan's was becoming too much of a habit. His three years on Mars were beginning to show.

The jail wasn't in the brick part of the Authority building, but in the complex of pneumatic architecture that sprawled behind it. The huts were old—older than his own—but dated back to the days when governments had not begrudged a few billions for exploration, back before space had to show a profit. For that reason, they were sound and well insulated, though a bit tacky looking.

The jail consisted of two huts joined together, one for offices, the other for the two makeshift cells and storage. Ferris was the only one there when he walked in, a young kid, younger than he had been himself when he had come to Mars. He was still impressed enough with his responsibilities and had not yet been worn down by the grim realities to take his job in any way but seriously.

Ferris greeted him with a solemn, "Good morning, *sir*," with a stress on the sir. As a three year veteran of Mars, Ferris looked on his boss with more than a touch of awe.

"Anything exciting happen overnight?" McKernan didn't really expect much. A few fights in the saloon district, a knifing maybe if things got out of hand. Petty thievery, or perhaps not so petty. He looked at Ferris and saw a flash of excitement in his eyes that the younger man was trying hard to suppress in order to match the hard bitten image he had of his superior.

"Yes, sir. We've got a murder on our hands."

"Another knifing down at Thelma's?" he asked, naming an infamous saloon and bordello that figured in a quarter of all the police reports.

"No. A prospector was found out on his claim yesterday, over on the far side of Olympus Mons. He was shot, Inspector."

That was bad, McKernan thought. People on Mars weren't supposed to have guns. With the thin skins of most buildings and a hostile atmosphere outside that would support life exactly as long as you could hold your breath, they were dangerous, and not just to the targets. The Authority had made them illegal and the corporations had been more than willing to agree. They weren't easy to get—not something that could be picked up casually or made, like a knife. Even without the details it sounded like the work of a real criminal and not just a squabble over a claim or a woman.

"Okay. Let me have the report. I'll take a look at it."

He took the folder from Ferris who looked a bit crestfallen. He probably expects me to go rush off to the outside and track down the murderer like an Indian scout, McKernan thought. He'd learn in time. Mars was a big planet and a dangerous one, but because of its nature there were also very few places that a man could run to and none where he could hide indefinitely.

He was leafing through the report when he came to his door. For the thousandth time he read, "Inspector Erik McKernan, Chief Constable." Mother would have been proud, he thought sardonically. She had hated the L.A. cops like all the other residents of the barrio. He went through the door into the little cubicle that was his real home. There, sitting at his desk, he began to read the report, sketchy though it was, to look for some explanations.

2

He was still studying the report when his phone rang half an hour later. "Erik? This is David Powell." Powell was the Authority governor. "You aren't busy, are you? I've got someone that I want you to meet. Will you come up to my office?"

McKernan didn't like the governor, nor did he have much contact with the man except at budget time or when the pressure was on. "I'd like to beg off. Something important has come up. A murder out past Olympus Mons."

"If it's already happened, I think that it can wait a little for you to solve it, Erik. I'll see you in a few minutes, then." The phone hung up before he could offer either acceptance or rejection. McKernan didn't like Powell, but he was his boss and as disenchanted with his job as he was, he wasn't ready to give it up yet. He'd have to go up and see what the old boy wanted.

The governor's office was in the solid part of the complex where the walls were made of painted-over brick. He was a political appointee, and on Mars, politics meant the corporations which in turn meant money. For Powell, the post was a form of exile, but it was far from an uncomfortable one.

McKernan was waved in by the governor's secretary, a good looking woman who knew it and kept only to high class company. He had tried more than once to get her attention, but when he entered the office his thoughts of the secretary vanished.

Sitting in a chair facing the governor was a young woman, obviously straight from earth. She was tall and lean, with long ash blonde hair and a tan that could only have been gotten under the home planet's skies. She was dressed in what must have been the latest style on earth, clothes that were neither worn nor patched. She wore them as if they had been designed for her. She looked rich, and sitting where she was, she was also important. The governor was not in the habit of seeing nobodies.

While still admiring her aesthetically, McKernan thought to himself that this was going to be a big pain. As if he didn't have enough problems, he'd have to put up with whatever it was that this woman wanted. She was probably a spoiled bitch whose father owned one of the companies that ran Mars, out for the thrill of life on the frontier. Well, he'd have to suffer with it if he wanted to keep his job. At least the scenery was nice.

"Ah, here's Erik, now," the governor said, noticing his presence. "Miss Olafson, I'd like you to meet Inspector McKernan. Erik, this is Miss Olafson. She's with World Press Agency. She's here on Mars as a guest of the Authority to do a series of feature articles on us."

They both made the perfunctory nods and noises. She made McKernan nervous with the way that she sat there sizing him up. It was different from the way that most women looked at a man. He decided that she was too self assured for his tastes.

The governor, in an effort to prevent the ensuing silence from becoming hostile, broke in. "You should be flattered, Erik. Miss Olafson has expressed a desire to write about your department, and about you in particular. I suppose that she fancies you in the role of a latter day western lawman. I don't know if we can live up to expectations, but I've promised her our fullest cooperation."

The latter admonition was obviously meant for him. He'd have to make the best of it. He only hoped that it would not take up too much of his time, especially with the murder investigation facing him.

"Well, I don't want to keep either of you," the governor continued. "Why don't you show Miss Olafson around. She's just come in on the last ship and hasn't had a chance to make herself familiar with our city, yet."

Taking their cue, they left the governor's office. McKernan was trying to think of a way out of showing the reporter around when she said, "We can forgo the guided tour, if you'd like. I would like to talk to you, though, if you can spare the time. I realize that administrators don't always understand the need to get things done. The governor is a lot like my editor."

Maybe she wouldn't be so hard to get along with after all, McKernan thought. She had sense and at least some tact and consideration. He thought it over for a minute and said, "There's a bar just around the corner. We can go there and talk. You'd have to catch the place sooner or later, anyway. It's kind of a local landmark."

She agreed and they found themselves in one of Finnegan's back booths. The bar was still almost empty, it being too early for the lunch crowd. Finnegan had raised his eyebrow when they had walked in, but McKernan couldn't decide whether it was because he had come back so soon, or because of the company he was keeping.

"This place is really amazing," she said. "It could be a bar out of the last century in the States or Britain."

"Wait till you taste the whiskey. That'll dispel any illusions. Strictly a local product. Finnegan distills it himself. He guarantees that it's at least a month old."

They ordered, and he was surprised when she ordered her whiskey straight up. He was more surprised when she downed it without choking.

"You're right, the whiskey is terrible. It's as bad as any G.I. hooch I've had out in the field."

"What's a nice Danish girl like you doing drinking hooch?"

"I'm Norwegian, not Danish, and I've been a war correspondent in both Paraguay and Burma. You learn to disregard the niceties when you're running around the jungle with people shooting at you."

"Touché, Miss Olafson. I was in Burma, myself."

"Call me Helga, please. I want you to know that I'm a competent journalist. I've worked as a reporter and photographer in combat zones, in Antarctica, and on the moon. I've got good enough sense to listen to people who know more than I do, and I don't take needless risks. But I do want to get this story, and I do intend to go wherever I have to in order to get it. I'd like to have your cooperation, if possible, Erik."

"Fair enough. If you don't get in the way you can tag along with me. If that's what you really want, that is. This job is a lot like police work anywhere. Most of the time it's routine. The only dangerous thing is the environment, though that's dangerous enough for anybody."

"That's fine. That's really all I want to do, to follow you around for a few days. To see how your job resembles that on earth, and how it's different. What the governor said about this being a frontier is a cliché, but it is true. That's the feeling that I want to capture for my readers."

"Okay. You know your business better than I do." He glanced nervously at his watch. "I've got some paper work to go over this morning, but I should be free after lunch. Seeing as you've just come in, you probably aren't settled in yet. Why don't you do that and then meet me at my office about one."

"That will be fine, and thank you, Erik."

————————————

One o'clock found McKernan at his desk finishing off the remains of a soyburger. He had waded through the day's paperwork, mostly arrest reports stemming from fights in bars and the ensuing damage claims. He had also written a request for more money and staff, something that he did with regularity every quarter. With equal regularity the Authority administrators on earth turned down each request on the grounds of tight budgets and more pressing needs at home. And every year the corporations operating on Mars claimed record profits.

He had also had a chance to reread the report on the murder and check on some of the details via a phone link to the far side of Olympus. The victim, a long time prospector and miner named Bill Morrison, had been found dead on his claim by another prospector, Toshiro Kuroti. He knew both men vaguely, and both were legitimate as far as he knew. Kuroti had placed a call to the mining camp at New Klondike and informed the constable there. The constable had told Kuroti to leave everything as he had found it, and then he had filed a report. The cause of death had been a bullet wound. There had been no signs of either a struggle or a robbery. Alexi Constantin, the constable at New Klondike, had nearly a quarter of the planet to patrol and he was content to leave all the investigating to his boss. McKernan decided that on this one he'd have to go out and look for himself.

He was on the phone making arrangements for a plane when Helga Olafson walked in. She had changed into a pair of well used jeans and a sweater which did nothing to hide her charms. An expensive but worn camera and a couple of lenses hung from her neck. McKernan finished his call, deciding that he was going to enjoy his duty as tour guide.

"I'm not interrupting anything, am I? I'm sure that I can find someone else to show me around."

"I'm afraid I can't allow that, Helga. The governor was quite specific about my responsibilities," he said with a smile. "There's nothing so pressing that Ferris can't handle it. If there is, he can always get a hold of me," McKernan said, indicating the two way, hand held radio on his desk. "Actually, I was just arranging transportation for a little trip that I've got to make tomorrow. If you want to see a bit of the planet, that would be a good opportunity for you."

"I'd love to. What I've seen of Mars so far isn't much different from Antarctica or the moon."

"Good. I'll make the arrangements. Do you have a surface suit?"

"No. I'd thought that I'd rent one for the time that I'm here. I understood that that was possible."

"It is. Rental suits are okay for tourists taking a jaunt on the surface close to the city, but if you're going to the outback that's another matter. Remember, your life depends on your suit, and you may be a thousand kilometers from help. Mars is a big place."

"I'll take your word for it that I need a good suit," Helga said without either deference or annoyance. "Where do I get one?"

"I know a place in hut town that's reliable and not too expensive. We can stop there as part of the tour."

"All right. That sounds fine. I'm ready whenever you are."

McKernan hooked the radio onto his belt and escorted the woman out of his office. He didn't spend much time on the sights of Main Street, just pointed out the important offices. His tour of the power plant and air station were nearly as brief. Helga didn't seem to mind much. She took a few pictures, but that seemed the extent of her interest.

"What about this hut town?" she asked finally as they were returning down the corridor from the observatory. "You say it as if it were a separate community, almost a ghetto."

"In a way it is, both physically and psychologically. It's a collection of huts, most of them used and discarded, that are neither owned nor controlled by either the Authority or one of the corporations. The Authority provides only minimal services which the residents have to pay for. It's held together more by the ingenuity of those who live there than anything else. A lot of the buildings are twenty years old or more, and they were designed to last maybe ten."

"It doesn't sound too pleasant."

"Parts of it aren't. Some of it is given over to whore houses and flops for miners and prospectors in town for a fling. But there are other parts that aren't so bad. The people who don't work for either the Authority or the corporations live there because they can't afford anything else. Most of the small businesses are there, too."

"It still sounds like a precarious existence. Can't the Trust Authority do anything about it?"

"How much do you know about the way Mars is run?" McKernan asked.

"I researched quite a bit before I came here, but most of the information was from the Trust Authority. Why don't you give me your version?"

"Okay, though this may take me a while. Originally Mars was just a scientific outpost. It was set up under a U.N. charter, but each nation took care of its own operation separately. The U.S., Russia, the E.U., Japan and a couple of other countries all had stations here. It was run a lot like Antarctica was before they started mining coal. There were only about a thousand people then, mostly scientists and their support, and it was all run on a friendly basis."

"It might have gone on that way, too, if it hadn't been for the discovery of large deposits of rare earths and other non metallic ores close to the surface. As you know, most electronics these days are based on semiconductors, especially exotic ones like gallium and indium. They're used in integrated circuits, lasers, all sorts of things. The important thing is that they're used in small quantities and that they are very rare and expensive."

"On earth they're produced as a byproduct of other mining, mostly for copper and lead. The amounts produced are small and the cost is high. There just isn't enough to go around, either. But on Mars, because of some freak of geology—probably because the planet is so much smaller and lighter—these elements are more concentrated, and they are near the surface where they're easily mined. And because they are so valuable—as valuable as gold or silver—it became economical to mine them on Mars and ship them back to earth."

"When the discovery was made, the mining rush was on. This was about twenty five years ago, just about the turn of the century. There was a big debate over who had the rights to mining. No country was willing to let another claim sovereignty, and a lot of the under developed ones thought that the planet should be held in trust for them. For a while it looked as though it might not be opened up for mining at all, but then the demand for those elements was so high that it had to be opened."

"An agreement was finally reached whereby private corporations would be allowed to develop specific claims, but administration of the planet would be put in the hands of the United Nations. That's how the Trust Authority was born. The Authority administers the claims and collects a tax on all products shipped to earth for the purpose of helping out developing countries. The corporations pay for the cost of the Trust Authority's operations, but in addition, it provides for a good part of the budget for most of the U.N. agencies. It's contribution is about equal to that of the U.S. and Europe combined."

"In principle it isn't a bad agreement. It probably prevented a war from happening—a real war, not a police action like Paraguay or Burma. But the corporations pay for the Authority, and the Authority monitors the corporations, and they both look after each other's interests pretty well. None of the corporations will make waves because the others are ready to back up the Authority against them, and no one corporation has that much pull with the Authority."

"There's only one problem. No one worries too much about the people who don't work for either the corporations or the Authority like the independent prospectors and miners or the people who came to Mars with one of the corporations but decided to try and make a living on their own when their contracts ran out. For the most part the corporations ignore them. The board that governs the Trust Authority is selected by the U.N. and the U.N. is mostly interested in getting its cut out of Mars. The corporations are the ones who pay the taxes, not the independents, particularly if they aren't miners."

"And so they get herded off to hut town?" Helga asked. To McKernan's surprise she had been following his lecture closely, taking notes in a little book she carried.

"Not consciously. It's more a matter of benign neglect. The corporations provide dormitories for their employees, the Authority does the same for its people. As far as they're concerned, that settles the matter. Everybody else is on Mars at their own risk and they have to look out for themselves. The Authority is run on a tight budget and there isn't much left over for those outside the system. The city provides utilities like water and air, but the hut towners have to pay for them, and they don't have any say on how the things are run."

"Most of them try to figure out ways to do without those services as much as possible. They'll buy up the cast offs from the corporations and use them to build their huts. They grow plants for food and air, they save their wastes to make methane and fertilizer. Anything to save a few bucks. Mars is an expensive place to live if you have to pay for it yourself."

"It sounds like a hard place to live," Helga said sympathetically.

"You said it, yourself. This is the frontier, and these people are pioneers. They accept the hardships. And it doesn't have to be such a bad life. Anybody with a little cleverness or good business sense can make a living here. It still costs a lot to ship anything from earth. Anything that can be made on Mars at all can be made cheaper than it can be brought here. Even the corporations are willing to buy products from some of the independent businesses if the prices are right."

"You sound like you admire these people."

"I do. Most of them are pretty good people. They know what they want and they are willing to work to get it. It's not like it is back on earth where a lot of people live on welfare just because it's easier. Here people have accepted responsibility for their fate."

McKernan had talked himself out and for a while they walked down the corridor in silence. They had been in hut town for some time in a district of small shops tucked back behind airlock doors. For the moment the doors were swung open so that the interiors and their goods were on display, but they were all ready to be closed on a moment's notice.

"Here's a good example of private enterprise, Martian style," McKernan said, stopping before one of the airlocks. A hand lettered sign above the portal said, "Surface Suits, George Goldschmidt, pro." "You can get suits on earth, but they're expensive and not really tailored for conditions here. George makes suits that I would trust my life to. I mean that literally. I own one. No one makes them better. Let's see if he can do something for you. Okay?"

"You're the expert."

Inside, the shop was a welter of pressure suits, air tanks, helmets, and air tight cloth, all of it stashed in such a way that it was doubtful that there was any order to it. Some of the garments were new, but many showed the signs of wear. With all the clutter, there was hardly space to stand except for a small clearing in front of three mirrors set up as in a tailor's shop.

Towards the rear wall of the hut there was a partition reaching almost to the ceiling. They could hear a rustling behind the partition and in a moment a small man of Semitic features popped out through a curtained doorway.

"Inspector. Good to see you again. You're not having any trouble with your suit, are you?"

"No, I brought you a customer. Miss Olafson is going to be taking a trip with me to the outback, and she needs a good suit. Nothing fancy, but reliable. If anything happens to her I'll come get you for murder." The last was said with a laugh, but there was an undertone of grimness in the policeman's voice.

"Erik, you wrong me," Goldschmidt said, the hurt in his own voice only half feigned. "When has one of my suits ever failed unless it was the owner's stupidity. Never fear, young lady. As you are a friend of the inspector's I'll be especially careful. And quick. I can have one ready in a week."

"That's not good enough, George. She needs it tomorrow by morning. We have to go out past Olympus."

"It can't be done. Not even by me. After all, I'm not Goodyear. Even if I dropped everything else it would take me four days." The little man looked thoughtful for a minute and then said," I've got a used suit that I've been reconditioning. The former owner was about your height, though she was built a little differently. I could have the alterations ready by ten tomorrow."

"What happened to the former owner?" McKernan asked suspiciously. At first, Helga had followed the conversation closely, but as she had been left out of it she had turned her attention to the shop and the examination of its contents. Pulling out her camera she had nodded questioningly at Goldschmidt who gave his assent. She began to take pictures while the two men talked.

"The owner returned to earth. She couldn't make a go of it. The suit is really in excellent condition. She worked at the observatory and didn't really use it much. It's got a Swiss regulator. Very good. It's machined to such tight tolerances that it doesn't need any lubricants. It won't freeze up when it gets cold."

"Okay. Let's see it."

Goldschmidt looked around, scratched his head for a moment and then dove into a pile in the corner. He handed the suit to McKernan and then began a search for the helmet. This took longer, but in the end he came up with it."

"All the electronics are Japanese. First class all the way. No problems with this suit," Goldschmidt said proudly, handing the helmet to McKernan.

"What do you think?" McKernan asked Helga as she took a picture of him.

"It looks all right to me. If you think it's a good deal," she said with a shrug.

McKernan nodded. Goldschmidt held the suit up to Helga and then began to take measurements with a tape measure that hung forlornly around his neck. He seemed to be enjoying his task as he wrapped the tape around her.

"You know, I came out to Mars twenty five years ago. I was an instrument maker with an expedition from CalTech. Mars was a different place in those days, and the suits weren't nearly as good. Hold still, please," Goldschmidt said as he laid the tape across her breasts.

"When it came time for the expedition to return I was asked to stay on at the observatory. So I did. I was in love with a girl who worked there. I've never been back to earth since." He made a measurement of the suit, tugged his tiny wisp of beard, then took another measurement.

"It's a funny thing. My grandfather was a tailor. He started when he first came to America from Poland. My father was a brain surgeon. He'd never forgive me if he knew what I was doing. He was upset enough when I became an engineer instead of studying medicine. But my grandfather, I think that he'd understand and be proud of me."

"Well, I've got all that I need," the suit maker said, though he hadn't taken one note of any of his measurements. "Now as to payment. Five hundred and eighty dollars in U.N. script."

"That's robbery, George. I ought to arrest you," McKernan said. "Helga, you can pay in U.S. dollars, can't you."

"Sure. The Bank of America has my line of credit."

"Okay. She'll pay one hundred and twenty five dollars American."

"You'll make me a pauper. Not less than two hundred seventy five.

"One fifty."

"Two fifty."

"Two hundred."

"Done. You can pick it up tomorrow at ten, Miss Olafson," Goldschmidt said, showing no rancor from the bargaining.

Later as they were walking back towards Main Street McKernan said, "It's getting late. Can I buy you dinner?"

"I'd love to, Erik, but the governor insisted that I dine with him tonight. I'm sorry." McKernan mumbled his acknowledgment. Helga added, "But I'd like to buy you dinner tomorrow. Don't worry, I can put it on my expense account. I've seen the prices they charge at the hotel."

"It would be my pleasure," the inspector said, sounding smug.

They walked along in silence for a while before Helga asked, "What ever happened to the girl the suit maker was in love with? I didn't see any sign that he was married."

"He isn't. He's never talked to me about it, but I heard the story from someone else, another old timer from the observatory. She had an accident about two months before she was to marry George. Her suit failed, which wasn't uncommon in those days, and she died. George never found anyone else as far as I know. Women have always been in short supply on Mars. I guess her death was one of the things that turned him to making surface suits. His don't fail, you can depend on that."

3

After dinner, McKernan returned to his office. He was in a depressed mood because he had had to eat alone. He tried to tell himself that it was only because women of any kind were in short supply on Mars, but he had to admit that he liked the Norwegian reporter. He knew that he shouldn't allow himself to fantasize, but he did anyhow. It didn't improve his mood any.

Gaeretts had replaced Ferris at the desk. The night man was an old hand on Mars, an ex-prospector who had given up that life for the certainties of a job with the Authority. He was a sound man, and McKernan valued his experience, but his manner was often less than deferential.

"How's the tour guiding go?" Gaeretts asked, looking up from his sandwich as McKernan came in. "Ferris said she was a real looker."

McKernan responded with a grunt that didn't invite further discussion on the subject. "Anything happen while I was out?"

"No, it's been quiet all day. But then it's still early. Things won't be getting lively down at Thelma's for a couple of hours yet. There's a good crowd of miners in town, so we might see a little trouble."

The inspector answered with another grunt. Gaeretts raised his eye brow, but shrugged it off. "I read Kuroti's statement. Morrison was a good man, not the kind that causes trouble. I've known him for a long time. We came out to Mars about the same time. Last time he was in town

I talked with him. He said that he'd struck something good out past Olympus. Do you think it was claim jumpers?"

"I don't know what to think. Kuroti's statement was pretty sketchy. I'm flying out there tomorrow to bring back the body and check over the scene."

Gaeretts looked thoughtful for a minute. "Be careful. I don't like the smell of this one. Whoever shot Bill could be waiting to take a shot at anyone poking his nose around in it."

"Don't worry," McKernan said. "Look, if things get hairy tonight, give me a call. Ferris is still a little green to back you up in a pinch. I'll either be at home or at Finnegan's."

"Didn't make out with that reporter woman, huh?" Gaeretts called out to McKernan's back as the inspector left the office.

4

McKernan was going over the morning reports when Helga Olafson showed up in his office. She was wearing a tight fitting jumpsuit of the type usually worn under a space suit. It revealed her figure admirably, and he let the sight sink in for a while before greeting her. "I see that you've prepared yourself for our outing," he said finally, referring to the surface suit she carried. "Did George check you out in it."

"Yes. He was quite thorough about making sure it was a good fit. More than was necessary. He seems to be as appreciative of my body as you are," she replied in an amused tone.

"George takes his work very seriously," McKernan said. "So do I, but you have to realize that good looking women are a rarity on Mars. Speaking of which, how did you survive the governor?"

"Just barely," she said with a laugh. "I had to tell him that I was an expert at unarmed combat to get him to say good night. You might have warned me."

"I thought you could take care of yourself," McKernan said dryly. "Are you ready to go?"

"Any time you are. I've got everything I need," she said patting the camera case hanging from her shoulder.

"Good. Just let me pick up my gear and we can go out to the hangar." He got out the bag containing his own surface suit, and then unlocking a cabinet in the main office pulled out a worn but reliable AR 16 carbine. He stuffed a couple of clips of ammunition into his bag before relocking the cabinet.

Outside in the corridor Helga asked him, "Is that thing really necessary?"

"Probably not," he replied. "Whoever shot Morrison should be long gone. But there has been a murder, and I'm not going to take any unnecessary chances. The governor would never forgive me if got you shot." After a pause he added, "And I'd never forgive me if I got me shot."

She realized he was more serious than his bantering tone let on and was silent the rest of the way to the airport.

The airport was nothing more than a large level plain that they reached by traveling through one of the inflated corridors. When they reached the final air lock McKernan helped her on with her suit, checking all the fittings and making sure that she was familiar with all the procedures. He then donned his own suit and explained the workings of the lock.

"Never assume that there is pressure on the other side of a door," he lectured. "This is Mars, and you might end up breathing a rather thin mixture of nitrogen and carbon dioxide."

The lock finally cycled and they stepped through. McKernan started towards one of the hangars, but Helga paused where her feet first touched the sand. Through the plastic of her visor McKernan could see her eyes staring out at the too near horizon, then looking up at the pink sky and the too small sun.

"It's different being on the surface. Like being on another planet." Realizing what she had said, "That must sound pretty absurd."

"It's true," McKernan said. "This is another planet, and all the rules have been changed on us. Don't feel ashamed. I've been here for three years and it still effects me that way sometimes. Especially when I'm away from the city. You'll see what I mean when we get where we're going. This area is tame compared to the outback."

He pointed toward the hangar and they started to walk across the pebble strewn field. Helga noticed the wire rope strung between posts about hand high that stretched out towards the hangars. "That's in case of sandstorms, so you can't get lost. They can blow for days sometimes, and the visibility is reduced to zero," McKernan explained.

"Cheery," was Helga's comment as her eye ran over the horizon.

The hangar was nearly a kilometer out from the airlock, but they adopted the long, half hopping stride used in low gravities and covered the distance quickly. As they approached the hangar Helga observed that it bore the insignia of the Anglo Martian Mining Company.

"Yeah. We'll be using their plane. The damned things cost a fortune, too much for the Authority. Even the corporations don't use them for much except shuttling around key personnel and running surveys. We have an agreement by which the Authority can requisition whatever is available in an emergency. Most of the corporations are pretty good about it. It's in their best interests."

The hangar was little more than an enclosed space which provided protection from wind and sand, but in front of it sat a low squat plane with an enormous wingspan, a wingspan far wider than the hangar. "They fold back for storage," McKernan said.   "I'll check her out with the mechanic and then we can go."

A man was already walking out towards them, his surface suit bearing the logo of Anglo Martian. "Plane's all ready for you, Inspector," came a voice with a midlands' accent over the suit radio.   Through the visor of the mechanic's helmet they could see a big bushy moustache above a set of smiling teeth.

"Thanks, Arthur. Any bad weather out Olympus way?"

"Not a thing," he answered as his eyes wandered towards Helga. "Right good looker, that one, Inspector."

"This is Miss Olafson, Arthur. She's a reporter from earth here to do a story about life on the last frontier," introduced McKernan wryly.

"Nice to meet you, miss."

"How many of these planes are there, Arthur?" Helga asked.

"There were six until last month. Nelson smashed one up running a survey for the Arabs. It's a coincidence mind you, but he was flying out the way you'll be going. But don't worry, miss. This one won't crack up. I take care of her myself, and the inspector, here, is a bloody fine pilot. Excuse me, miss. We don't often get good looking women from earth out here."

"Well, we'd better get going if we're going to get back in time for that dinner you promised me," McKernan said.

"Just sign here, Inspector. She's all fueled and ready."

McKernan signed out the plane and then walked around it to give it a quick visual inspection. Satisfied, he helped Helga up through the tiny airlock in the fuselage. The plane was a dull black, its aluminum skin pitted from years of exposure to wind driven sand. Owing its origin more to the high altitude spy planes of the cold war than to any commercial aircraft, it was long and narrow with long slender wings. For take offs and landings they stuck straight out to the sides, but during high speed flight they could be sharply swept back. Instead of wheels it had skids for an undercarriage, and downward pointing rockets that would let it land and take off from any short, fairly flat, stretch of sand. Twin rocket engines tucked in close to the tail could propel it to nearly three times the speed of sound.

Climbing through the cramped cargo hold, McKernan led his companion to the cockpit and indicated a seat for her to take before he began his preflight check. As he had expected, everything was in order. He pressed the button that ignited the two main thrusters underneath. The plane lifted to a height of about ten meters and began to drift forward out of the shadow of the hangar. Satisfied that all was working he opened the throttles. The plane leapt forward leaving Helga gasping at the acceleration. Because of the thin air, the plane gained altitude slowly. Only when they had reached cruising altitude did the wings sweep back so that the plane could go supersonic.

Despite a speed of 3000 kph they were flying at a much lower altitude than they would have on earth due to the thinness of the atmosphere. The sensation of speed was much greater than it would have been on earth because of this and Helga spent the first few minutes of the flight with her face pressed against the plastic of the cockpit canopy.

"I had thought that we'd be going by some sort of tractor," she said finally. "I hadn't really thought about planes on Mars. It's a lot different than flying on earth."

"If we'd gone by marsbuggy we'd still be traveling next week. It's over twenty five hundred kilometers from the city to where we're heading. These planes are the only thing that enables the Authority to do any sort of effective policing on this planet. You have to remember that the surface area of Mars is just about equal to the total land area on earth. Even with the planes for emergencies, we're stretched pretty thin."

"Just how many men do you have to cover the planet?"

"There's ten plus myself," he answered. "Actually four of them are assigned permanently to the city. About forty percent of the population lives within fifty kilometers of there.   All the Authority offices and the corporation headquarters for everybody but the Russians. That's also where all the prospectors and miners come to blow off steam. That's where most of the trouble occurs."

"That leaves six men to cover the rest of the planet. They're mostly based out of the larger mining camps so that they each serve about the same number of people. They try to make the rounds to as many places as possible, but that still usually leaves a lot uncovered. We never know half of what goes on in the outback. We were lucky to find out about this case.   Another prospector happened by Morrison's camp within a couple of days of the murder. If he hadn't, we might not have found out until someone reported Morrison missing, and that might have taken months. He'd just gone back out after filing his claim and getting some supplies."

While he had been talking, Helga had gotten out her cameras and was taking pictures through the cockpit window.   McKernan lapsed into silence for a while concentrating on his flying. The rockets provided only a muted roar from far to the rear, and any wind noise there might have been was left far behind by their speed. It was easy just to let the surface pass by underneath them.

"Where did you learn to fly, Erik?" Helga asked after she had shot off a roll of film. "It can't be a common skill on Mars if planes are so expensive."

"I flew jets in Burma during the war. I wasn't too happy about it then, but I guess it helped me get this job. That and the law degree I got after I was discharged."

"This is a long way from Burma. Or law school, for that matter. Why did you take this job? You said yourself that life on Mars isn't easy."

"Yeah," he said with a touch of bitterness. "I ask myself the same question all the time, but it's really pretty simple. I got my degree, but I wasn't quite good enough. That and I didn't have any contacts. My parents were working poor. I probably never would have made it all the way through school if it hadn't been for my G.I. benefits."

"You know what things are like on earth. Especially in the U.S. There are a thousand applicants for every decent job, even the indecent ones. I wasn't quite good enough. I spent a year and a half looking for work after I got my degree. I filed an application with the U.N. for another job, but when they saw that I could fly and had taken some criminology courses in addition to the law degree they asked me to apply for this job. I was better qualified than anyone else at the time. There weren't many applicants."

"It was either this or settle for some clerk's job if I could have found one. It paid well and I was getting desperate. So here I am my own boss and a half dozen grades higher on the promotion scale than I could have hoped for on earth. I get hardship pay and in twenty years I'll be able to retire on a fat pension."

"You sound like you're not sure you'll make it."

"Mars is a dangerous place. My predecessor lasted less time than I have before he got careless. But I plan to do my damnedest to collect that pension. I'll still be under fifty then," he said wistfully.

"You sure ask a lot of questions," McKernan commented.

"You forget, I'm a reporter. It's my job." McKernan acted as if he wasn't sure that that was the answer he wanted. The rest of the flight was spent in small talk with McKernan pointing out landmarks on the surface and explaining about the plane and his job. Helga continued to take pictures from her seat behind the pilot.

When they were about an hour out McKernan started to consult a map, comparing it with a visual inspection of the terrain below. "We're in luck," he said as he powered the plane back for descent. "There's a nice flat place only a couple of kilometers from where we're headed. We can hike it if you're up to it."

"I'm willing. I've done some walking on the moon. The low gravity shouldn't bother me."

"Good. We're going in now." He cut back on the throttles some more and cut in the thrusters to compensate for the loss of lift. To Helga's eyes the plain below didn't look very inviting for a landing. It was strewn with pebbles and rocks up to the size of a soccer ball and was less level than McKernan had promised. The plane seemed to be falling too fast, but a hundred meters from the surface the descent checked itself and they came to rest with little more than a bump.

"Okay. Button up good," McKernan said as he checked Helga's equipment again.

"I think I can manage," she said, bristling a bit at his attention.

"It's easy to forget something when you're fresh on the planet. Even people with experience forget. Last year a miner died because he went out and forgot to fasten his faceplate. He'd been out here five years."

Outside, McKernan tied the plane down attaching it to stakes which he drove into the ground. "It would be embarrassing if the plane should get flipped by a sudden wind. Even if it wasn't fatal." Satisfied, he opened a door in the skin of the craft and pulled out two packs. He handed one to Helga and pulled the other one on himself.

"Survival gear," he said in answer to her inquiring look. "We won't be out long enough to use it, but I never take chances. I've seen what happens to those who do."

They set out across the plain, but soon found themselves climbing a slight grade up into rougher terrain. McKernan was worried at first about Helga's ability to take the strain of walking in the low gravity, especially encumbered as she was by the surface suit and the pack, but his worries soon turned to admiration as he watched her lean body gracefully go through the almost balletic motions that are the most efficient means of locomotion on planets with low gravity.

5

The going got progressively tougher and it became clear that they were climbing a ridge. They were forced to circle around a rock mass to avoid a climb of some fifteen meters. At last they came to an escarpment where they could look down into a wash, one of the curious erosional features found on a planet that had long since been desiccated. Down in the bottom of the gully they could see Morrison's camp.

Before making the descent, McKernan signaled that they should take a break. Helga took advantage of the opportunity and brought out a camera with a telephoto lens and began taking pictures of the camp. McKernan was less concerned with the camp for the moment than he was with the surrounding rock faces. He scanned the sides of the wash with a pair of binoculars. As far as he could tell they were alone.

Turning the binoculars on the camp below he surveyed the scene. In a flat spot in the wash perhaps two hundred meters away was the temporary shelter that Morrison had set up along with the equipment he had used in prospecting. A short distance away a balloon tired van had been parked, its trailer still attached. A set of tracks not yet filled in with sand ran up the wash towards the east.

Both the van and the hut seemed to be undisturbed. The building was still inflated, and all the gear next to it seemed to be reasonably orderly. There was another set of tire tracks running through the wash, but McKernan assumed that they belonged to the vehicle that Kuroti had been driving.

The only thing out of place in the scene was a tarpaulin lying between the hut and the van covering some lumpy object. Rocks had been placed on the corners to hold it down against the wind. McKernan knew that underneath lay Morrison's body. Kuroti had covered it up after finding it, but had otherwise left it untouched.

"Okay. Let's go down," McKernan said. Helga noticed that he had unlimbered the carbine and held it loosely in his right hand. Nervously she glanced around her, but then the descent took all her attention. The slope was not great, but the side of the wash was unconsolidated material that had a tendency to slide out from underneath their feet. The descent was more of a controlled skid rather than a climb.

"Don't touch anything until I give the okay," McKernan ordered as they approached the body. "I would appreciate it though if you could take some pictures. They might prove useful later on."

"Just tell me what you want them of," Helga answered.

The inspector let her take some shots of the body and the van before he moved in. Kuroti's footprints were still visible. The sides of the wash had served to protect the spot from much of the wind. From the looks of it, Morrison had been unloading the supplies he had bought on his last trip to the city. A crate stood upended next to the body where he had dropped it.

When Helga gave him a nod indicating that she had the pictures he moved closer and lifted up the tarp. The sight wasn't particularly pretty. Morrison was lying face down. There was a small hole in the back of the helmet of his surface suit, the plastic of the helmet crazed in a pattern of cracks around the hole. Below in the sand was a pool of blood that had congealed in the cold and low pressure.

He turned the body over. It was frozen stiff, and not just from rigor. The floor of the wash was in shadow most of the day and the temperature was far below zero. There was no face. The tiny hole in the back of the helmet had broadened into a cavity as big as his fist. The entire front of the skull had been blown into fragments. He could see bits of bone and tissue laying in the sand where the force of the bullet had hurled them.

He had purposely kept his body between Helga and the corpse. "It's pretty gruesome. It might be better if you didn't look, but I should have a picture of this."

"I've seen bad wounds before. In Paraguay and Burma," she said a little defensively. They both knew what Burma had been like. He stood aside holding the tarp so that she could see the body. She blanched, but took the picture anyway.

"I've seen wounds like that before. It looks like a high powered rifle with a soft nosed bullet," Helga said finally standing back from the body.

"I think that you're probably right about that. Almost like a hunting rifle of fairly high caliber. I would have sworn that there wasn't a gun like that on the planet. There isn't anything to hunt." He knew it was unlikely that the murderer was still around, but he eyed the walls of the wash uneasily. "He must have sat up on that ridge over there waiting for Morrison. It looks like he had just gotten back from getting supplies. He was still unloading. He just sat up there with his rifle and a scope waiting for Morrison to show. He might have been waiting for days, living in his suit and an emergency tent. He waited until Morrison showed up, got ready, took aim and then pegged him. One shot, and to the head. Not a high percentage shot. He must have been awfully sure of himself."

"I don't like it, I don't like it one damn bit. It's too bloody professional. This was all planned out well in advance. It was a set up. You don't get a gun like that on

Mars. You can't hardly get a gun at all. It must have been smuggled in special from earth. I sure hope so. I'd hate to think of somebody sitting up here with an arsenal like that."

He dropped the tarp back over the body and started to pace around. To Helga it seemed as though he was taking the murder as a personal affront. After a moment he said, "I'm sorry. I just don't want this sort of thing to start happening here."

She looked at him questioningly. "There really isn't much crime on Mars, not big crime. Little thefts yes, that sort of thing. And fights over women or money. Sometimes even a killing. But this is different. I'm sure of it. This wasn't the work of just one man. Not with smuggling that gun up here."

"What do we do now?" Helga hadn't liked the sight of the wound, but McKernan noted that she wasn't letting it get to her. He was showing more of a reaction than she was. Well, he thought, she'd probably seen enough in Burma, and not from twenty thousand feet, either. She was a steady sort, not like most of the women he'd met.

"I want to look around some more," McKernan said in a calmer voice. "See if I can figure out any motive. It doesn't look as though anything was taken. Then I'll bag up the body and stuff it in the van. We can drive back to the plane. There's a place where the wall of the wash is pretty shallow about two kilometers up that way. It's the long way around, but with the van it shouldn't take us that long."

There wasn't much to see. There were some signs of digging, but if Morrison had struck it big it hadn't been close to his camp. Most of the excavations looked as if they were six months old or more. It was hard to tell if any of the mining gear or supplies had been touched, but there wasn't anything obvious. The inside of the hut was almost antiseptically neat. Morrison had been a tidy housekeeper, but that wasn't surprising. He had had a lot of time to himself with nothing to do, and the old time prospectors tended to be very careful. That was how they got to be old timers.

It was well past two, and McKernan wanted to get back while he still had light. Getting the body in the plastic bag he had brought for that purpose wasn't easy. The limbs were stiff and it was an awkward handful. Finally Helga held the bag while he maneuvered the corpse. He hadn't asked her. She had just picked it up.

He stuffed it into the cargo compartment in the back of the van, then they went through the airlock into the passenger compartment. There was still plenty of fuel and the turbine fired up easily when he started it. He gave Helga the sign that she could remove her helmet, but they didn't do much talking on the way back to the plane. There didn't seem to be much to say.

The sun was close to setting when they made the approach to the airport, the shadows of the hangars long and distorted, the sky an intense, cloudless pink color that only a Martian day could possess. The flight had been depressing. Helga hadn't even brought out her camera.

After McKernan had checked in the plane he escorted her to the tunnel entrance. He was uncertain whether she still wanted to dine with him that night, but inside the airlock she smiled and said, "I need a little time to clean up and dress. Why don't you meet me at the hotel bar around eight thirty."

"That sounds fine," he said trying not to sound relieved. "Do you think you can find your way home from here? I've got a few details to attend to." They both knew that the "detail" was Morrison's body, but neither wanted to bring that up. She nodded and disappeared down the corridor.

Later, McKernan headed back to the office. On the way back he had started to formulate a plan for solving Morrison's murder. It wasn't much of a plan, mostly checking up on Morrison's background and the last trip he had made into the city. He was dissatisfied with it, but with the few leads that he had there wasn't much choice. As he passed Finnegan's he thought about stopping in, almost tasting the bite of a cold glass of beer on his palate, but he decided against it. He knew that he was drinking too much and that this night of all nights he wanted to keep his head clear.

Ferris was still in the office when he walked in, though he should have been off duty and hour earlier. Gaeretts was there, too, the remains of his dinner on his desk. "Anything important turn up while I was out?"

It was Ferris that answered, "No, it's been a real quiet day. No problems at all."

Gaeretts broke in, "I just got word of a knifing over at Interplanet's mining camp five. Not too serious, just a flesh wound. A little too much booze it looks like. Other than that, it's just like the kid said, all quiet."

Ferris winced at being called the kid. "What did you find out at Morrison's?"

"Not a hell of a lot. Mostly Morrison," McKernan answered. "He was killed with a high powered rifle, probably from a kilometer or more away. There wasn't any bullet that I could find, no clues. That's about it. But seeing as you're still here and so eager, Ferris, you can take care of the body. It's out at Anglo Martian's hangar. Take it over to the hospital and have Doc Schweitzer run an autopsy on it."

After Ferris had left Gaeretts said, "That was a rough one to pull on the kid. I don't imagine the corpse is very pretty."

"He's got to learn sometime," McKernan said, "and facing a week old corpse that's frozen is easier than facing one just dead."

Gaeretts nodded. He could tell that his boss wanted to talk about the case, but didn't want to start the conversation himself. "It doesn't sound like we have much to go on."

"We don't. About the only thing we know for certain is that Morrison was killed with a rifle. My guess is that it was a hunting rifle. Not too common on Mars. If we can find the rifle we stand a good chance of finding the killer. I don't think that there's a gun like that on Mars legally, but I want you to check and make sure. Also, check up on anyone who was a hunter or marksman on earth. Check service records, company personnel files, anything else you can think of. Kaminski can take your shift for the next few nights or so while we check this one out."

He paused for a moment waiting for Gaeretts to comment. When he didn't, McKernan continued, "This guy was good. Too damned good. One clean shot through the back of the head. He didn't go for the easy shot to the body. Even with a telescopic sight it was good shooting. I don't think I could do that well in a surface suit."

"What if I can't turn up any gun or marksman?"

"I don't know," McKernan answered. "Try to figure out a motive. As far as I could see, nothing was taken at Morrison's. There was a van all loaded down with supplies at the camp. Twenty thousand worth easy, not counting the van, so robbery is out. Maybe something to do with Morrison's claim. You knew Morrison, and some of his friends, too. It wouldn't hurt to ask around, maybe check what he did and who he saw the last time he was in town."

"I can see that I'm going to be busy," Gaeretts complained lightly. "And you'll be escorting that Nordic bombshell while I'm working my head off, I suppose?" McKernan grunted. "Will I be able to get you at Finnegan's if anything should break tonight?"

"No. I've got a dinner engagement at the hotel. I don't know how late I'll be," McKernan answered.

"You're doing better than I thought. I didn't know you had it in you, lad," Gaeretts called out as his boss left the office.

6

Except for a few desiccated examples of Martian geology and a collection of photographs of the more spectacular pieces of planetary scenery, the bar of the Mars Hotel didn't look as if it belonged on Mars. Instead, it looked like any of its equivalents on earth. It had bad lighting, small tables, and a decor that could have been stamped out of a mold. The white jacketed bartender was too busy doing his job to be really friendly, and he wore a smile that was as plastic as the counter behind which he worked.

McKernan never went there unless it was on business, and it wasn't just the tourist prices that kept him away. The place made him uncomfortable. The neighborhood that he had been raised in hadn't been a slum, though it had undoubtedly become one, but it had never been the residence of the wealthy. He had never become used to manifestations of wealth and power. Only the rich tourists and the top men in the corporation and the Authority could afford the Mars Hotel, and McKernan knew that he didn't qualify as a member of either group. Six years in the Air Force hadn't made him an officer and a gentleman; Burma hadn't been that kind of war. Now he was a cop and he knew it.

Helga was sitting at the bar when he arrived. She was wearing something filmy and white which covered just enough skin to make it interesting. It set off her earth tan and blonde hair perfectly. He was wearing his best jacket, the one he had brought out from earth, but he still felt awkward and ill at ease. The bulge of his shoulder holster underneath didn't help any.

Helga smiled at him when he sat down next to her, her green eyes big and lovely. "Order anything you like. My editor is the one that's paying for it."

He called the bartender and ordered bourbon, the real stuff from Tennessee. He took a sip when it came and savored the taste of it. It had been a year since he had last tasted real earth whiskey, when an executive from one of the mining companies had tried to bribe him. He hadn't been bought, but he had drunk the man's whiskey just the same.

Helga was already at work on a double of scotch, neat. "This place reminds me of the Holiday Inn in Council Bluffs. Except for the prices, that is. Twenty eight dollars a shot is a bit on the steep side even for a hotel bar."

"Tourists on Mars aren't people who worry about money. Everyone else in this place is either on an expense account or getting a healthy hardship allowance from the Authority. All the important people in the corporations stay here. It's the only place there is. It's the same with the Authority, from the governor down to department heads."

Her attention perked up and she scanned the room. "Anybody particularly interesting?"

"Most of them are tourists," he said. He looked the place over unobtrusively with a policeman's eye. "The fat, bald one at the end of the bar is the local manager of Interplanet. The man with the goatee in the corner is United Semiconductor's chief geologist. That's his secretary with him. She's not as dumb as she looks. With the pay out here they can attract both beauty and brains." He looked around some more. "The man in the rumpled suit who looks like he's had one too many is the distinguished head of the Mars Institute. He's smarter than he looks, too. He's spent the last two years drinking up the better part of a Nobel prize. Normally he drinks at Finnegan's, but every once in a while he comes here for a change."

"Do you know everyone on Mars?" she asked.

"The important ones. That's part of my job. It's not that hard, really. Mars is a pretty small place, and the faces don't change that often." As he finished his attention was caught by a man at the rear of the room sitting facing the door. He was well dressed but very conservatively. He didn't look like a tourist, but McKernan couldn't place him as one of the corporation men or scientific staff from the Institute or the observatory. Possibly he was just being suspicious, but he decided to have Ferris check him out in the morning.

The waiter called them and they finished their drinks. The menu was covered with items with three digit price tags, though there were home grown dishes that cost less than the shot of bourbon he had had. He passed up the more exotic dishes and settled for a filet of Martian trout.

Helga raised her brow but ordered the same. "Martian trout? I thought that they hadn't discovered any native fauna?" Helga asked in puzzlement.

"They haven't," McKernan replied with a smile. "The trout are of the earth variety. A prospector came here about five years ago. He hit a strike, but not a big one, and he decided that wasn't where the money was. So he bought some surplus fuel tanks and had some fingerlings shipped from earth. He raises them in the tanks. He raises catfish and lobster, too, and he is going to try salmon if he can figure a way to get them to spawn. They're still damned expensive, but they're a lot cheaper than food shipped from earth."

"I noticed. I thought that two hundred dollars was a high price for a T bone," Helga said.

"Small animals like fish and chicken aren't too difficult to raise here," McKernan continued. "Quite a few people have them out in hut town. Even a few pigs. But cattle are a different matter. They eat too much, and it has to be grain which is expensive when everything has to be grown indoors. There was some talk about one of the corporations doming over a crater and converting it into pasture, but nothing has come of that yet."

"You're kidding about enclosing a crater," Helga said, "aren't you?"

"It was a small one. I've heard of crazier schemes that have been pulled off up here. Even if they did do it, though, it would be a long time before you could buy much beef. They'd probably keep it all for the big men in the corporations."

They had aquavit after dinner, Danish, and McKernan had to admit that it was very good. The scent of the brandy and the woman were going to the inspector's head as much as the alcohol. A three piece band began to play, and they danced once on the tiny dance floor, but neither of them were good dancers. Helga suggested that they go for a walk.

The lights of the main corridor had been turned down to simulate the night outside and to save energy. They walked silently, but Helga had taken his hand when they had left the hotel. She showed no inclination to be taken back to her room. McKernan was wondering how the night would turn out when he saw Gaeretts running towards one of the airlocks leading towards hut town.

"There's a couple of miners trying to carve up the place at Thelma's" Gaeretts replied to McKernan's question. "It sounds pretty serious. The bartender called me."

"It must be serious if the bartender is calling in. I'd better go with you." Turning to Helga he said, "I'm sorry, but I'd better see to this. Can you see yourself back to the hotel?"

"Oh no you don't," Helga protested. "I don't want to miss this. I came out here to see the action, remember."

McKernan hesitated a moment, then saw the anxious look on Gaeretts' face. "Okay. You can come along, but stay out of the way. And watch yourself. This could be dangerous. Thelma's is a pretty rough place even when there isn't a fight going on."

———————————

Thelma's was a saloon far out on the fringes of hut town. Originally the big pressurized building had served as a warehouse for one of the mining companies. Now it was the cheapest, loudest, and most disreputable of the colony's entertainments. Most of the clientele were prospectors and miners who came in for a few days every six months to blow off steam and get new supplies. Fights were common, though few resulted in serious injuries. It took a degree of skill and practice to be lethal in the low gravity.

The three made their way up the North corridor, stopping only to open the periodic airlock doors. Most of the corridor's buildings served as storage, with a few having been converted into flophouses for visiting prospectors. The corridor itself was empty, which suited McKernan just fine. The last thing he wanted was a crowd gathering to watch the fight.

The saloon was marked by an ordinary airlock crowned by a garish neon sign that sputtered as it flashed. Gaeretts led the way, elbowing aside the crowd that had gathered in the lock. They gave ground reluctantly, glaring at the constable, but when they saw McKernan behind him, they parted to let him through.

Once inside it was apparent that more than a pair of miners were involved. A space had cleared in the middle of the floor in which five men stood facing each other. Two men, one with a knife, the other with the remains of a chair, were up against three others, two with knives and the third with a broken bottle. McKernan recognized the two underdogs as a couple of fairly successful prospectors who had never caused much trouble before. That was more than he could say for their opponents. Two of them he knew to be miners at United Semiconductor's No. 3 camp. He had run them in a couple of times before, and once they had busted up this same saloon. The third he didn't remember, but he looked no better than his companions.

Gaeretts had pulled out his blackjack and was bellowing at the combatants to break up the fight. The two prospectors backed off, looking relieved at having the fight stopped, but one of the miners rushed Gaeretts while his back was turned. He got the cosh across his jaw for the trouble.

The biggest of the remaining miners closed in on the constable, but McKernan moved in to head him off. The miner grinned and the bottle neck flashed wickedly in the beam of a spotlight on the ceiling. Instinctively the inspector reached for his boot knife, drawing forth the hands breadth of steel while he sized up the other man. The miner was taller and heavier than McKernan, and he made his living hauling around mining machinery instead of sitting behind a desk. McKernan, however, figured that he was the faster of the two and not nearly as drunk.

The miner lunged forward bringing the bottle around in a wide arc aimed at McKernan's midsection. McKernan wasn't there, though, sidestepping easily. There was a trick to hand to hand combat on Mars where the gravity was only a third of the earth's. Muscles grown on the home planet were likely to force one to overshoot. Either man could easily have lifted the other clear of the floor, so muscles alone wouldn't be of much worth unless they closed in and grappled. The inspector wasn't about to do that.

The miner's face had gone red from anger and frustration at having missed the policeman. He hadn't learned his mistake, though. He came in again with a wide arm swing as before, but this time McKernan ducked underneath, lifting the miner up as he got behind him and spilling him on the floor. He kicked out to knock the bottle away, but the miner, suddenly sobered by the fall reached out and knocked McKernan's leg up, forcing the policeman back.

McKernan avoided taking a tumble, but the miner had time to regain his feet. McKernan was wary, now. The miner held the bottle point up. He wasn't going to take anymore round house swings. He glanced over at Gaeretts, but saw that the other was busy subduing the third miner. Suddenly the bottle was coming up at him in a move that would have eviscerated McKernan if he hadn't stepped back. The miner swung again at the off balance policeman, the tip of the glass raking across his stomach.

The cut burned, but McKernan concentrated on the bottle and the wrist wielding it. The miner had been unable to check his own momentum and had kept turning after the swing. McKernan brought his doubled fists down hard on the miner's back as he pirouetted in front of him and then as the miner fell he grabbed the outstretched arm with the bottle. He brought the arm down hard across his knee.

The bone snapped suddenly and the bottle was released to float to the floor in a gentle arc. The saloon had become hushed. McKernan still held the miner's wrist as Gaeretts handcuffed it to that of the third miner. The other one was still out on the floor.

The inspector turned to the two prospectors and said between panting breaths, "I want you two in my office tomorrow morning before ten o'clock to see if there are any damages, then I want you out of town and I don't want to see your faces for a month. I'll take your knifes until then." The two men handed over their weapons reluctantly, though McKernan figured they each had another stashed in their boots.

To Gaeretts he said, "Take these others to the hospital and get them patched up, then throw them in the jug. Call United Semi's personnel man and tell him I want all three of them off planet on the next ship out. Don't release them until he shows up with their tickets. Do it tonight, but wait until you're sure the personnel man is asleep."

He reached for his knife where it had fallen and stuffed it back in his boot top. It was only then that he noticed Helga on the edge of the crowd, a compact camera in her hand. Now that the excitement had died down she stood out in that crowd and some of the miners were eyeing her hungrily. He grabbed her arm and led her out into the corridor. "Don't you ever stop working?"

"Do you?" she said half in anger. Then turning serious she asked, "Is all your justice so cavalier? You never even asked who started the fight."

"I knew most of the men involved. I've had run ins with a couple of them before. Besides, the big one went for Gaeretts. He got what was coming to him. We don't try to do more than stop fair fights unless they draw blood. We'd have to bust half the miners on Mars if we did any more. But trying to stab a cop or an unarmed man is something I'm not going to put up with. I don't buy that stuff about an offenders rights, not when he's got a knife pointed at me."

Helga was about to protest further when she noticed the tear along his flank. "You're hurt."

He reached into his shirt and his hand came out smeared with blood. "He must have tagged me with that bottle. I didn't even feel it until now. It's not serious. I'll patch it up when I get home."

"No you won't. I'll do it. I'm taking you home right now and fixing that cut."

McKernan started to object but then gave up. "Okay. I'm too bushed to argue. It's been a long day." She smiled at him and he thought that things weren't working out to badly after all.

7

Helga insisted on supporting him though he didn't really need her help. The wound wasn't that bad, especially under Martian gravity. She raised her eyebrow when he led her through the airlock into the south corridor, but she didn't comment. Nor did she say anything when he opened the airtight doors of his own hut.

It was cold inside, and her thin dress didn't offer much warmth, but she sat McKernan down on the cot and helped him out of his jacket. With alcohol and a cotton swab from the first aid kit on the wall she washed out the wound. Without his shirt McKernan was cold himself and he winced at the bite of the alcohol on the cut. The wound was ragged, but not deep. The bleeding had stopped so Helga sprayed it with an antiseptic and taped it over.

"You'll live," she said when she had finished. "Your shirt is in worse shape than you are. If you have a needle and thread I'll sew it up for you."

He pointed at the cabinet with his sewing kit and then watched as she sat at his table mending his shirt. Her nose wrinkled as she concentrated on the stitching. The incongruity of the scene forced him to smile and when she finally looked up she caught the look on his face. She tried to resist her own impulse, but finally put down the shirt laughing.

"Quite a domestic scene, isn't it?" he asked. "Famous war correspondent and frontier marshal. At home after a hard day's work."

A strange look passed over her face as if she were making a decision.   She asked, "Are you making a proposition?"

"The cot is kind of narrow for two, but it's not as hard as it looks. Low gravity is good for some things."

When McKernan woke his side was throbbing from the wound. Spending the night in the cramped cot hadn't helped it any, but he wasn't sorry. The hut was as cold as ever, but with the warmth rubbing against him he didn't mind as much. He tried not to wake her, but she turned to face him and hugged him while shivering. He winced, but put his arm around her and held her for a long time.

"I'm sorry it's so cold, but the heating unit doesn't work too well. I keep meaning to fix it, but I just never have the time."

"I've slept in colder places. And with less agreeable company. But tonight I think we should sleep in my hotel room. It's warmer and the bed is bigger."

"And have people talk," McKernan said mockingly. "What about your reputation?"

"You drag me off to a fight in some run down saloon, and then you worry about my reputation." She embraced him again but stopped when he winced. "Does it hurt?"

"Only when I laugh," he answered, which produced a groan from both of them. McKernan glanced over at his clock and said, "It's time for me to get up and go to work."

He started to dress, choosing his clothes from those stuffed under the cot. She looked seriously at all the hardware he carried but said nothing. As he washed and shaved she got up and pulled on a sweater from the pile on the floor. Then she poked around his kitchen area and by the time he was done McKernan could smell a pair of soysteaks frying.

He sat down at the counter beside her and began to eat. Despite the fact that she hadn't combed her hair and was dressed in a sweater several sizes too big for her and nothing else, she looked very desirable. It had been a long time since he had thought about a woman in that way, since before the war when he had been a college student. He'd have to watch himself.

Helga seemed to think nothing about sitting in the chilly hut eating a soysteak while half dressed on a planet thirty five million miles from her home world. She ate with a good appetite, wiping up the grease with a piece of bread.

Without warning she asked, "Why are you called Inspector?"

"Why not. It's as good a title as any."

"But with you being the inspector and your men constables it's like something out of Scotland Yard."

"They had to call us something. The U.N. wanted to avoid military ranks. There was quite a debate about it, I understand, though that was before my time. None of the nations wanted to use the titles of another. It was actually suggested, by the executive of one of the American companies—from Texas I think—that it be marshals or rangers. I think that was what finally settled them on inspector. The companies figured that marshal had too much of the flavor of the wild west about it. It was too raw and unbusinesslike. Only the Russians objected to the English ranks, and they got outvoted. So Inspector McKernan it is."

She laughed at this story, and at that moment McKernan wished that he could stay there with her forever. But he couldn't do that, not with a murder to solve. He knew that

Helga had work to do also, and neither one of them was the type to shirk duty.   He drank his coffee, for once not minding the bitter taste of the tepid liquid.

"What are you going to do today?" he asked as he showed her how to wipe the plates clean using sand.

"I've got an interview at the observatory this morning," she answered wrinkling her nose. "My editor doesn't send a reporter to Mars every day, and he's determined to get as much mileage out of me as he can, so in addition to my main story he's asked me to do some science stuff and some human interest pieces, if I can find any."

"You don't sound too happy about it," McKernan observed.

"It's not really my kind of thing," she shrugged.   "I'm used to action and excitement. I like new and strange places. There's not much of that left on earth these days. That's why I took this job, and that's why I like it. You're the same way, otherwise you wouldn't be out here on Mars."

"I don't know," McKernan said softly.   "Sometimes I think I could do with a little less excitement. Maybe I'm just getting old, but I like things nice and settled."

"Mars is a funny place for that, isn't it?" she asked with a touch of sarcasm.

"Maybe, but it's not always going to be a frontier. There are a lot of people trying to make it their home and a good one. I'd like to think that I'm helping them out."

"You are, Erik, you are," Helga said. She glanced at her watch then took a quick look at the clock sitting next to the cot. "Which one of these is right? I've got an appointment at the observatory and I don't want to be late."

McKernan laughed, then explained, "Your watch is still set for earth time. The day on Mars is about half an hour longer than it is on earth. We stick the extra time in between 12:59 PM and one in the morning. All the clocks are adjusted accordingly. Just set your watch back half an hour every day. Thirty seven and a half minutes to be precise."

"Convenient of you Martians to put the time in the middle of the night. We'll have to put that extra time to good use tonight. Still, I'd better get dressed if I'm going to make that interview."

"I've got to get to work, too, but I'll walk you to the hotel if you'd like," McKernan said. He watched her as she dressed unselfconsciously before him. He wondered if that was because of her Scandinavian upbringing, or whether she really felt that comfortable with him. She certainly didn't seem to question the fact that they would be sleeping together that night.

———————————

She kissed him when he left her in front of the hotel and she promised to meet him for lunch at Finnegan's if she could get through her interview. He found it was important to him that she would.

Ferris and Gaeretts were both in the office when he arrived, the latter looking tired. Gaeretts had a stack of printouts spread before him and another stack sitting on the chair next to his desk. He looked up as McKernan entered, a quizzical look in his eye.

It seemed as though he were going to make a remark, but Ferris spoke first. "I took the body over to the hospital like you told me. They didn't seem too happy about it, but I told them it was your orders. I've got the doctor's report here."

"You didn't have to make them work in the middle of the night. After all, the body had been out in the cold for a couple of days at the least." Ferris had a habit of being overeager and McKernan found it a bit trying. He took the report from Ferris and began to read it.

"The cause of death was a bullet to the posterior occipital region resulting in massive trauma. Great, he was shot in the back of the head and had his brains blown out. I already knew that," McKernan said in annoyance. There was a lot more in the report that was mostly technicalities, but towards the end he found what he was looking for. "It is impossible to judge for certain the time of death due to the interval and the condition of the corpse. However, judging from the extent and depth of crystallization of the cells within the body, the best estimate is that the victim was killed four to five days before recovery."

Gaeretts had been listening to McKernan read the report. "I talked with a couple of Morrison's friends and the outfitter that he got his supplies from. He left here on the fifteenth. It would take him about ten days to get out to his claim. That would be five or six days ago."

"So he got shot about the time that he arrived at his claim," McKernan said. "That's what it looked like. He was still unloading his van from what I could see. Well, at least we have some idea of when he was killed. That should help us eliminate some suspects. Anything turn up yet on the rifle?"

"If that rifle exists on Mars it's not here legally. Not even the Russian's will admit to having anything like it, and lord knows what they keep over at Novya Magnetogorsk. But legally, the only long range weapons on the planet are in that rack over there," Gaeretts said, pointing towards the weapons' cabinet against the wall.

"As far as marksmen goes, well, that's another story. I haven't had a chance to check with all the corporations yet, but from what files I've been able to get from them and the

Authority so far, there are at least six or seven hundred men who have spent some time in the military or in some sort of reserve training. Any one of those might have had the training."

"The man we're looking for is an expert," McKernan said. "He wasn't just somebody who knew how to shoot a rifle. He only took one shot and he made it count."

"Yeah, I know, but that's just not the kind of records that we have available up here. I've sent some inquiries back to earth, but it may be weeks before we get anything—if we get anything at all. Some governments aren't exactly free with military information when it comes to the U.N. I'm afraid that the same holds true for hunters or people who have held hunting licenses. Let's face it, nobody keeps a record of hunting licenses on Mars. There isn't any reason to. I'm trying to get the personnel men to ask around, but I doubt that our murderer is going to go out of his way to give us any help."

"Yeah. I had figured on as much," McKernan said. "Keep on digging anyway until you run out of things to check. We just might get lucky with something." Gaeretts gave a shrug and turned back to his papers. "What about those three that we arrested last night? Did you get in touch with the man from United Semi?"

"Yeah. He wasn't any too happy about being gotten out of bed at three in the morning. That really broke me up. He complained about harassment and exceeding our authority and a lot of other things, but they're sending a ship back to earth tonight. He said that he'd have all three of them on it."

"Okay. Release them into his custody, but not until just before takeoff."

"That's about what I told him. I checked up on those three when I made out the arrest forms. I found something interesting while I was checking their files."

He handed McKernan a flimsy sheet of paper, a photostat of the miner's employment record. McKernan glanced over it until he spotted what Gaeretts was referring to. The miner, named Joseph Penderkarass had served in Burma as a ranger. The record listed his years of service along with the notation that he had received a dishonorable discharge. McKernan raised his eyebrows and looked at Gaeretts who handed him another file, this one from the Authority Office of Immigration. The Authority didn't let just anyone come to Mars, though their standards weren't very strict. Evidently the discharge had been enough to raise a question about Penderkarass. The discharge had come in Burma where he had been charged with taking a shot at an officer. The man hadn't been hit and the case had been dismissed on the grounds that Penderkarass was too good of a shot to have missed, but a month later he had been cashiered from the service, anyway.

"I see what you mean," he said finally.

"I thought so, too, so I checked with the United Semi man. Penderkarass has got a solid alibi for the last week. He was on the other side of the planet at United Semi #1. Twenty men will swear that he was there all the time. No way he could have gotten around to the other side of the planet. The other two were with him as well. Do you still think we should send him back to earth?"

"If he's got that tight an alibi we really don't have anything to hold him on. I'd just as soon get rid of the lot of them."

Gaeretts grunted and went back to his files. McKernan turned to his office, but just then the two prospectors who had been part of the fight entered the station. McKernan motioned them to join him in his office.

The prospectors were physically dissimilar, one being six foot plus and blonde, the other a foot shorter and oriental, but they both had the lean, hard, and slightly crazy look common to men who spent a large part of their time in the Martian outback. After three months of living within the confines of a small pressurized dome or in a surface suit it was not surprising that men like that turned wild when they visited the city for a few days of civilization before returning to their claims.

McKernan's office didn't have an extra chair and he intentionally didn't offer the prospectors one. They hadn't caused much trouble in the past, but he wasn't about to encourage them. For whatever reason they had gotten involved in a fight with weapons, and they would at least have to bear some of the discomfort as a reminder that the Authority wasn't going to tolerate such things.

McKernan glared at them for a minute trying to look as though he was disappointed in them. He wasn't sure whether he succeeded, but Svenson, the blonde one, looked suitably sheepish. It was harder to tell with his partner Fokuda. Though born a fourth generation southern Californian, his Japanese features still lent themselves to inscrutability.

"The bill for damages at Thelma's comes to two hundred and eight in U.N. script. I want both you boys to pay up now and not come back into town for a month."

"Two hundred and eighty dollars!" Svenson said in outrage. "We only broke one chair, and that fell apart before I could really use it."

"So don't get into fights," McKernan countered unsympathetically.

"What about the others?" Fokuda asked quietly. "Are they paying their share?"

"For your information, the others are getting bounced back to earth. It's only because of your clean records that I'm not doing the same to you. Take your lumps and pay up."

"Be reasonable, McKernan. We didn't start the fight. Last night was our first night in town in four months, and when we heard about Morrison we decided to get drunk. His claim wasn't far from ours. We were just drinking and minding our own business when one of those miners, the one you busted up, picks on Akiro and tells him he don't like gooks and takes a swing at him. I blocked the punch and the next thing I know, his two friends are pulling out knives. We were just defending ourselves."

"We haven't had any time off in a long while. You can't just send us back outside after only one night in town," Fokuda complained. "That's inhuman."

"So is taking a swipe at one of my men with a knife," McKernan said. "But I'm willing to take your story at face value. If you pay for the damages I'll let you stay in town for two more nights. But you've got to stay out of trouble, and you've got to promise me you'll stay out of Thelma's. There are enough saloons in this town that you don't have to get drunk in the worst one."

"We'll stay out of trouble," Swenson said. "Don't worry."

"Good. I want you to check in here each day until you leave, and I'm going to keep your knives so you won't be tempted. You can pick them up when you leave town."

"Sure, McKernan, anything you say."

The inspector waved them out of his office, and then he tackled the paperwork on his desk, counting the hours until lunch.

8

Helga wasn't at Finnegan's. McKernan grabbed a stool at the bar looking dejected. He signaled to Finnegan for a beer and leaned into the bar. The beer would never have met the standards of Munich or Amsterdam, but the alcohol content was high. One thing the Authority hadn't been able to regulate despite all the pressure from the bureaucrats on earth was the local production of alcoholic beverages.

He would have liked to talk to Finnegan, but the proprietor was busy with a conversation at the other end of the bar. McKernan was trying to convince himself that Helga had actually been held up with her interview at the observatory when she walked in the door.

She grabbed the stool next to his and laid a sheaf of prints on the counter top. "I'm sorry that I'm late, but they have a darkroom at the observatory, and they let me print up some of my film. These are the pictures that I took out where Morrison was killed."

McKernan looked over the pictures carefully. They were good pictures. Helga knew what she was doing with a camera, and the sight of the body hadn't affected her work. But they still didn't provide any clues.

"They aren't much help, are they?" she asked when she saw the disappointment on his face.

"It's not your fault," he reassured her. "There just wasn't anything there to take pictures of—not that would do me any good. Forget it. Let's order, I'm hungry."

Finnegan came down and took their order, returning in a minute with a pair of sandwiches. He saw the pictures on the counter and commented, "Morrison, isn't it. Ghastly sight."

McKernan nodded affirmation. "He was in here last time he was in town, you know," Finnegan continued. "He said that he'd struck something rich. You hear that all the time from prospectors, but I think Morrison meant it. He'd been out here too long to get excited easily. He came in here one afternoon to celebrate. Bought a bottle of Chivas and sat here at the bar drinking it. Bought me a drink, too. The only time a prospector does that is when he's really hit it. It's a shame, you know. Morrison grubbing all these years looking for a real strike and then to get cut down just when he's found it."

"Yeah. I only hope that I can get the one who shot him."

"You will, lad. You will," Finnegan said before he went off to serve some customers.

"You don't sound too certain," Helga said. "Hasn't anything turned up?"

"I've got Gaeretts checking up on things, but there's no record of any such gun on Mars, and there are all too many people capable of using one. The only likely suspect we've turned up so far has an ironclad alibi. Unless I can find that gun I don't think I can crack this one."

"You don't like that, that you can't solve this one murder. It's more than just that you don't like to see somebody get away with something. It's a personal challenge for you. I can see that in your eyes. I've seen that look before, Erik. It's not healthy. Don't let this murder become an obsession for you."

"Don't worry, I'll survive. But you're right. I don't like this business, and as long as there is some chance of solving this case, I'll keep working on it."

He drank his beer and decided against another glass of the bitter brew. "What have you got planned for this afternoon?"

"I'm trying to arrange a trip out to one of the mining camps. I want to see if I can spend a day or two taking pictures and talking to miners. I've got an appointment with the manager of United Semiconductor's operation. The governor helped set it up."

"That figures. Old Powell is in pretty tight with that crowd. Maybe too tight."

"Are you jealous?" Helga asked.

"No, just suspicious," McKernan answered. "Powell isn't out here just for his health—or for the excitement of the frontier, either. United Semi put a lot of pressure on to get him appointed. Some of the other corporations weren't too pleased with the idea. But they were all bickering amongst themselves at the time, and so Powell got the job. He wouldn't be above taking a little squeeze if he thought that he could get away with it, but the stakes would have to be pretty high. He was in high rolling circle back on earth."

"Very interesting," Helga said, jotting a few notes in her notebook. "That's one of the advantages of sleeping with a policeman. You get all the gossip." She glanced at her watch and then at the clock behind the bar for confirmation. "Well, I've got to get going. Till tonight?"

"Okay. I'll take you out to dinner tonight. About seven?" Helga nodded and gathered up her things to leave.

When McKernan returned to his office, Ferris told him that the governor wanted to see him as soon as he came in.

McKernan did an about face and headed for the governor's office.

The secretary was more friendly than usual, but McKernan didn't notice. She buzzed the governor and then waved him in. Not for the first time McKernan wondered what the governor actually did. He never seemed to be busy.

Obviously, this occasion was not going to be as pleasant as his last visit to the office. the governor had on a carefully studied expression of sternness, one generally reserved for budget time when McKernan presented the requests for his department. It was still two months to that joyous event, so he decided that there must be something else on Powell's mind.

"I've been getting complaints about you, McKernan," the governor started without any preliminary pleasantries. Being blunt was an unusual action on the part of the politician, and the inspector was immediately on his guard. "There have been some pretty serious accusations of brutality raised against you and claims of very arbitrary and high handed conduct."

McKernan sat without being asked and looked impassively at the governor. The latter tried to stare back, but finally averted his eyes from the icy stare of the inspector. For a moment silence hung thick in the thin air of the room as if the governor was waiting for McKernan to defend himself. McKernan remained silent.

"Well," Powell asked finally. "What do you have to say for yourself? I'm not sure I like your attitude."

"First, I'd like to know exactly what charges have been brought against me, and by whom. There isn't much I can say, otherwise."

The governor might not have been expecting such a hard line from McKernan, but he didn't show it. Twenty years of politics had taught him that much. "All right. The most recent case deals with an incident last night. Three men were beaten and then arrested and now it seems that you have ordered them deported from Mars without a hearing of any sort, or without giving them a chance to defend themselves against any charges you might have."

"As provided for in the Authority charter," McKernan said. "The Authority and the mandate it operates under is not a government, it is an administration, and if in the opinion of the official charged with security, any person or persons within the jurisdiction of that Authority constitutes a menace to the safety of public order, they may be expelled on the judgment of that official. No hearing or judicial action is either specified or implied. I am that official and I have so judged."

"Don't play space lawyer with me, McKernan. Your action is costing United Semiconductor a great deal of money and that's not going to make them happy. They carry a lot of weight as I'm sure you are aware, and they aren't going to take this lightly."

"That is their privilege," McKernan replied. "If they don't like it they can lodge a protest with the Authority council. On Earth."

"Be reasonable, McKernan. This situation is getting blown out of proportion. United Semi brought these men to Mars at great expense, and the corporation needs them out at the mines. The Authority is here to promote mining, not to interfere with it. The corporations aren't going to stand still for having their best men sent back to earth. Now I grant you that these men may have started a little trouble, but what can you expect. After three months in the outback they deserve a chance to blow off a little steam. If you are willing to cancel the deportation order, United Semi is willing to call the matter closed. I think that is a reasonable compromise."

McKernan looked hard at the governor for a moment, trying to guess if Powell had been bought or whether he was just playing politics. In the end he decided that it didn't really matter. "I don't. These men are chronic trouble makers, and at least one of them has a record and should never have been allowed up here in the first place. As for blowing off a little steam, the two that got busted up committed acts of assault on myself and one of my constables. Coming at a law officer with the broken end of a beer bottle is not blowing off steam, it is a serious criminal offense in any country on earth. The Authority has no power to punish any offender, but under the charter it can expel any individual who constitutes a threat to public safety, subject only to the ruling of the Authority Council and the General Assembly of the U.N."

"I may not have the authority to countermand your expulsion order, McKernan, but I do write your fitness report, and I promise you that it is not going to be flattering. You may consider Mars to be your personal preserve, but it is not. You were appointed by the council, and you can be replaced by them. And if they do so, you can consider your career finished." Powell's voice had risen and despite the thin air, he was forced to wipe the perspiration from his forehead with the silk handkerchief from his jacket pocket.

"You implied that there were a number of complaints against me," McKernan said in a soft voice that did nothing to hide the stiff resolve underneath. "I think that I have a right and obligation to hear them."

From the uncomfortable look on the governor's face, McKernan was fairly certain that the complaints, if there were any, were not substantial. Powell, however, was saved from replying by the buzz on his desk intercom.

"Governor Powell?" the intercom sounded when he had depressed the key. "Is Inspector McKernan with you?" This, though there was only one exit from the office that was right in front of the receptionist's desk. "His presence is requested at the Claim's office immediately. The director said that it was urgent."

"You'd better go, McKernan," the governor said, regaining some of his composure. "We'll continue this discussion at a later date."

McKernan rose and left without saying goodbye. He did, however, compliment the secretary on her impeccable sense of timing. If she noted the sarcasm in his voice, she ignored it.

The Claims and Assay Office was not in the Authority building, and strictly speaking, it was not a part of the Authority, but instead was in another branch of the U.N. dealing with the resources of Mars and of the seabed and seeing to the equitable disbursement of the royalties that came from the mining of those resources. The two arms of the U.N. were somewhat jealous of each other, but McKernan had never had any part in the struggle.

The director of the claims office was a burly Jamaican who was well over six feet. He spoke with an incongruous Eatonian accent except when he was drunk or very agitated. He was neither at the present, but McKernan could tell from the set of his ebony face that he was concerned.

"Erik, so glad that you could come," the director said as he extended his hand and flashed a smile of brilliant white teeth. The smile was brief, but sincere. "Will you step into my office where we can talk?"

McKernan gathered from that comment that what the director had to say was not to be discussed in public. He followed the man into his office, glancing out through the plexiglass walls at the scales, chemical apparatus, and mass spectroscopes that constituted the assay portion of the office. Most of the white coated technicians were either dark or oriental in features. The politics of the U.N. were such that members of the developed countries were not trusted to oversee the world's common resources, that task being left to the citizens of the third and fourth worlds.

"What is it you want, Jack? I was told that it was urgent." The two men were not close, but they respected each other and their relations had always been cordial. McKernan did not think that the director had brought him down just to waste his time.

"You know that my department has always been above suspicion," Jones said as a preface. "It is important that it remain so. We have the responsibility for assigning and monitoring claims and conducting assays, and with the dollar amounts involved and the number of nations and corporations represented, it is of paramount importance that we carry out those responsibilities fairly and impartially."

"I've never heard anything but praise for you and your staff, Jack," McKernan said. It was not flattery, but fact. The man was skilled and diligent, and as demanding of his own people as McKernan was of his.

"It is not my staff that I am worried about," the director replied. "But I have reason to believe that someone has tried to tamper with the records we keep."

McKernan raised his eyebrow, but remained silent. "I came across it just by accident, but there is evidence that a file cabinet containing claim applications has been forced open."

"Could I see this cabinet?" McKernan asked.

"Yes, certainly. But I must ask you to be unobtrusive. You can understand what it might mean if word of this got out. Right now we enjoy the confidence of everyone, even the Russians, but if people suspect that the records had been altered it would throw the whole system of allotting claims into question."

"I understand," McKernan said. "But I still have to conduct an investigation if you suspect something like this."

"Of course. But it isn't necessary to mention our suspicions of a break in at this time. I have told my staff that you are here on an inspection of security measures, which, of course, in a way you are."

"All right. I'll go along with that for the moment," McKernan said with a smile. "Shall we inspect this file cabinet?"

Jones showed him into a narrow room lined with file cabinets and storage racks for mineralogical samples. The walls of the room were made of silica bricks twenty centimeters thick and closed off by a door made of plate steel that had cost a fortune to lift from earth. A combination lock was set in the center of the door and the locking bars were four centimeters thick.

"Is that door locked at night?" McKernan asked.

"Yes, always. I see to it myself. And at noon as well."

"And is there an alarm system?"

"Regrettably, no. Budget considerations you understand. Mars is not considered a high crime risk."

McKernan nodded and continued to examine the file cabinets. It wasn't obvious, but he could see the marks in the paint where something had been used to jimmy one of the locking pods. You'd have to be lucky or looking for it to spot it, but the marks were there. In his university days he had taken a course taught by one of the LAPD's experts on burglary. The man had opened up a cabinet similar to the one he was examining leaving just those kinds of marks, but that man had been an expert. An amateur couldn't have managed without leaving big gouges. He checked the other cabinets, but saw nothing. The burglar, if there was one, had either been extremely careful or very selective.

Back in the director's office McKernan asked, "Is there any chance that those marks could be old? They aren't very visible."

"I don't think so. I'm very particular. Perhaps too particular according to my staff. I think that they must have been made quite recently, say within the last week or so, though I can't say for certain just when."

"And there's no chance that one of your staff could have done it during working hours?"

"No. As you can see, the door and the interior of that room are visible from this desk. And I am here at all times when that door is open."

"And who besides you has the combination to that door?"

"No one. That is, none of my people. There is a copy on earth, and I believe there is one in your own files somewhere, but none of my staff has one. That does put suspicion on me, doesn't it?"

"Not really. You have a key to the drawer as well, I assume?"

"Yes, I see your point."

"Is there any way to check to see if anything is missing?" McKernan asked, amused at the mineralogist's missing of the obvious. "Could you hold an audit, and do you keep some sort of duplicate records?"

"Yes, of course," Jones said. "We keep a copy of everything on computer tape and a photostat as well on microfiche.   And copies of everything are transmitted to earth once a week. I'll start looking right away."

"You might start with claims filed in the last two weeks. Especially in the area just to the west of Olympus Mons."

Jones looked surprised at the suggestion but nodded. McKernan was satisfied. It just might be a coincidence, but when two very professional crimes occur within days of each other when no such similar crimes had happened in years, it made one suspicious.   And this job looked professional. Safe cracking wasn't a common skill on Mars. It was either that, or start suspecting Jones—which the inspector wasn't ready to do.

9

Helga was waiting for him at the hotel when he stopped by to pick her up. She wasn't dressed nearly as spectacularly as she had been the night before, but it was still a cut above Martian norms. They kissed briefly, but enthusiastically, Helga apparently accepting their relationship as lovers as being an established fact. McKernan did nothing to dissuade her.

Though Helga tried to pump him as to their destination, the inspector refused to divulge it, maintaining that it was a surprise. Exasperation and impatience proved to be of no avail, and so she followed him back into the tunnels of hut town.

As in all the businesses and residences in hut town, the entrance to the restaurant was made through the double metal doors of an airlock. This one, however, was distinguished by a pair of Chinese ideograms painted in red lacquer and gold leaf on a sign board next to the airlock. Helga's surprise was evident, but McKernan led her through the lock without a word.

If they were inside a pneumatic hut of aluminum and foam it wasn't apparent, for they found themselves in a small antechamber walled with paper screens. Moments later they were greeted by a small woman in a kimono. Of obvious oriental extraction, she bowed, smiled, then ushered them through one of the screens after politely indicating that they should remove their shoes.

There was no common dining room as such, only a series of small alcoves, each with a low table, and each separated from the others by screens of paper suspended by thin slats of wood. Helga was intrigued by the screens as they had been decorated with hand painted scenes and calligraphy. Though of a traditional style, the scenes depicted were of the Martian landscape, craters and boulder strewn plains set against skies of pale pink wash. Somehow, so portrayed, the Martian landscape looked neither as dangerous or forbidding as it did in real life.

"This place is amazing," Helga said after their hostess had left. "I would never have thought that Mars would hold so many surprises before I came here. First an Irish bar, and now a Japanese restaurant."

"It's actually more a combination of a number of oriental styles," Erik said. "The owner was born and raised in San Francisco. He came up here as a geologist. His wife worked for one of the Chinese cooperatives. This place started as a side line, but when it came time to return to earth they couldn't decide which country to return to. They ended up deciding to stay here."

His explanation was interrupted by their hostess and a kettle of steaming soup. She laid out utensils, ladled out two bowls of the mixture and retired, sliding the screen behind her. "There is no menu. You have to take what they're cooking that day, but it's always good. They grow most of their own vegetables in a green house behind the restaurant. Everything is a Martian product. No imports."

Half a dozen courses followed the soup, some traditional oriental cooking, some unfamiliar dishes, the quantities of each modest, but the variety almost endless. All were vegetarian. Strangely, for an oriental table, there was no rice.

"Growing any sort of grain on Mars is impractical," McKernan replied when asked about that singularity. "It just requires too much room and water. Vegetables are a much better proposition. You can get a higher yield of protein for the amount of resources put into the growing. Most people in hut town grow at least some vegetables if they can find the room."

"The doctors say that the diet of most Martians is pretty good for you, high in protein and low in fats. That and the low gravity lessening the strain on the heart muscles is supposed to give us a long life. I don't know about that. No one has lived on Mars long enough to find out. Most Martians are primarily vegetarians, but that's mainly a matter of economics."

The meal ended with a white, fruity wine. After the dishes had been cleared, Helga moved around to McKernan's side of the table where he sat on the mat flooring. She leaned against him with her glass in hand. For a long time they were silent.

"I'm glad that you brought me to this place, Erik."

"I thought that you'd like it," he said, pressing his cheek to her hair.

"You're rather proud of this place, aren't you?" Helga said after a moment.

"Yes, I guess I am," he said with a smile. "In a lot of ways this place represents the real Mars, the Mars of the future. There is nothing here that fights against the planet. Everything, from the menu to the decorations, is an adaptation to the environment. It's all home grown or home made. They grow their own vegetables. George made this table himself from wood he salvaged from a packing crate. Even the pictures were painted by Mrs. Wong."

"You couldn't do this sort of thing on earth," Helga said, "not today. You can't hardly find a decent Chinese restaurant, not even in Hong Kong or Beijing. The price of labor is too great."

"Even with half of the world's population unemployed," McKernan said with a touch of bitterness. "Earth had become too regulated, too complicated. In a lot of ways things are simpler here on Mars. You can do what your talents allow you."

"If you have any talents," Helga replied.

"Martians are pretty talented as a whole. There's a stiff selection process. It costs a lot to send someone to Mars. Only the best get sent. After that, the planet does its own weeding out of the careless or the stupid."

"That's pretty callous."

"Mars is a frontier. It's like any other frontier. Like my own country a couple of hundred years ago. Frontiers tend to attract the adventuresome."

"And the dispossessed and downtrodden. I think your parallel goes awry there. I don't see that happening on Mars. The people that I've seen so far all have skills and education."

"For every engineer here there are a hundred unemployed on earth. Mars isn't for the complacent. It's a hard and unattractive place when you've been raised on earth. But that doesn't mean that it will stay that way. They used to look at America as a bleak and forbidding wilderness in the 17th century. Time can change that if it's given a chance."

"And you're not sure that it will be," Helga said sitting up and looking at him, studying the lines in his face. He looked older and sterner. "Do you worry about the corporations?"

"Not as long as they don't get complete control. Mars needs the corporations. They bring in the money and the things that can't be made here. Most Martians live off the salvage from the corporations. If it wasn't for the mining we'd all die. The corporations are good for Mars as long as they don't squeeze out the independents, as long as they give them room to move and make a buck."

"And the Authority?"

"I think that the same can be said about it. It's not very responsive to anything except the politics on earth, but it provides a lot of needed services. And it helps keep the corporations in check despite the fact that it protects their interests. It doesn't take sides among them, and as long as there is competition no one gets too powerful. That's the thing that could ruin it, if one company got big enough to freeze out the rest. Then they'd freeze out the little guys, too. That would be the end. Just one company and the Authority to back them up."

"Can I quote you on this?" Helga asked.

"Are you still being a reporter?" McKernan asked.

"Yes. That's why I'm here, remember?"

McKernan wished that for a moment at least he could forget it. Finally with a thin smile he said, "Okay, except maybe for that last bit about the Authority. I'm afraid that I'm in a bit of hot water as it is, without criticizing the Authority in the papers. I had a row with Powell today."

"It's not serious, is it?" Helga asked, suddenly worried.

"I don't think so. Not unless the governor's got more clout back on earth than I think he does. He's on pretty weak ground as far as I can see. And I think that I've made a few friends that will speak up for me."

"Be careful, Erik. Politics is a messy business, and it's the good ones that suffer."

"So you think that I'm one of the good ones?" he asked reaching out to her.

"You were last night," she said coming to him. "Speaking of which, maybe we should go back to the hotel now. I've got to get up early tomorrow. I've arranged to go out to United Semi's Camp #3 for a couple of days. I want to see what life's like away from the big city." They both laughed at that. Softly she said, "I want to make the most of tonight. It'll be a couple of days until we can see each other again."

Helga's room at the hotel would not have been in the luxury class on earth, despite the prices her magazine was paying. It was more like a stateroom on a ocean liner, and one on the lower decks, at that, if any such vessel had still sailed earth's seas. It was small, unadorned, and there was a notice above the sink in the tiny bathroom that water was metered and its use would appear on the bill.

It was, however, warm, almost cozy, and its main feature was a real bed with clean sheets. Helga wasted no time. After closing and locking the door, she crossed to McKernan and began to undress him. She had some trouble with the shoulder holster and the inspector took over, placing the hardware on the nightstand next to the bed, where it would be within easy reach. He pulled back the covers and laid down waiting for her to undress, watching the fluid movements of her body as she slipped out of her skirt and sweater.

She came to him, pressing him down against the sheets, covering him with her body. They kissed for a moment and then she reached over to the lamp. There was very little conversation after she turned off the light.

The light was on when he woke and he could see by his watch on the nightstand that it was past seven. Helga was sitting on the end of the bed checking her cameras and putting film into her camera bag. He watched her as she worked with careful precision, checking each lens, dusting it off, making sure that everything was in working order. It seemed perfectly natural to him that she should be nude.

She frowned at a speck on the glass of one of her telephoto lenses, her forehead wrinkling as she tried to blow it off. Satisfied at last, she packed the lens in its case, then looked over her shoulder at McKernan.

"You're awake," she said matter of factly. She packed the lens carefully back into her bag and then crawled up the bed towards him. They made love briefly, but not without passion, coming to climax quickly and then resting in each others' arms.

"You're not happy about my going, are you?" she asked. "I can see it in your face."

"I can't say that I am. I'm going to miss you."

"I'll miss you, too, but I'll be back in a couple of days."

"Be careful. I don't want anything to happen to you."

"Are you jealous? Afraid that I might meet someone else? You don't have to be."

"No, that's not what I'm worried about. A mining camp can be a dangerous place, and I won't be there to protect you. So take care of yourself. If you get into any trouble, give me a call. There's a microwave link out to Camp #3 and they can always patch me in on my two way."

"You make it sound so ominous. I'm a big girl and I can take care of myself," Helga said bristling slightly.

"I'm sure that you can, but I've got a bad feeling. Camp #3 isn't that far from where Morrison was killed, and a lot of strange things have been happening out that way lately."

"Don't worry. I'm sure I'll be all right. There'll probably be a dozen people around to protect me at all times. Now I've got to get dressed. I'm supposed to catch a plane out there at eight thirty and it's already past eight."

"You're watch is fast. Remember, Mars has twenty four and a half hour days. You've still got an hour and we still have time."

"I'm sure you arranged that extra half hour on purpose," she said sinking to the sheets.

"It is convenient," McKernan added.

10

On his way to the office McKernan stopped in at Finnegan's for a quick one. It was the first time in three days that he had stopped in before lunch, something of a record for him in recent months. Finnegan smiled at him as he came in and poured a shot from the private bottle he kept behind the bar.

"I was beginning to think that I had lost your custom, Inspector," he said as he passed the glass over the bar. "Have one on the house." McKernan lifted the glass and sipped at the whiskey.

"It's the woman, isn't it? Had a fight?" Finnegan asked without McKernan speaking.

"No, but she's left town for a couple of days. I'm just beginning to realize how much it matters to me. I should know better than to get involved. She'll be returning to Earth eventually. There's nothing to keep her here."

Finnegan raised his eyebrow at that. "No, perhaps there isn't, Inspector. But as to not getting involved, you know better than that. Getting involved is the only way to live life. The ones who don't get involved are home on earth watching the telly."

A nice bit of philosophy, but there's no future in it. I keep wondering that if I feel so lousy when she's gone for a couple of days, how am I going to feel when she's gone for good?"

"You're vulnerable, Erik. You've met the first real woman that's come along in a long time and she's affected you. That's only normal. Maybe it won't last, but enjoy it while you've got it. If you'll take a bit of advice from an older and wiser man, the only thing worse than dwelling on the past is dwelling on the future. It only spoils the present."

McKernan smiled and downed the rest of his drink.

––––––––––––––––

Ferris and Gaeretts were already at the office when he arrived, the latter with a grin on his face. The ex-prospector seemed to have an inside track on all the gossip on Mars; a handy trait for a policeman, but an embarrassing one when the gossip concerned his boss.

"Anything turn up yet?" McKernan asked ignoring Gaeretts expression.

"Not so far. Penderkarass has the most likely record, but he also has an airtight alibi. No one else comes even close to being as good a suspect, though there are probably a couple of hundred men who have the technical capability."

"Speaking of Penderkarass, did those three get off on time?" McKernan asked.

"Yeah. I turned them over to the United Semi personnel man myself. The ship took off for earth at nine o'clock last night. Two weeks from now they'll be back on earth. The personnel man wasn't any too pleasant about it, but I told him that he didn't have any choice."

"Yeah, I know. I got a lot of flak from the governor about the expulsion order yesterday. United Semi put on a lot of pressure, and you know what side Powell's bread is buttered on. Well, keep looking until there isn't anything more to look at. We've got to try to do something about this case."

Gaeretts grunted and turned back to his files. "Anything else I should know, Ferris?" McKernan asked as he got a cup of coffee from the office pot.

"Jack Jones from the Claims office called. He wants you to return his call as soon as possible. Other than that there's just the morning arrest reports. It was a pretty quiet night."

McKernan took the arrest reports and carried them into his office where he dropped them on his desk. Jones answered his call and said that he wanted to talk but that he didn't want it in either of their offices. The man seemed worried and excited at the same time. McKernan agreed to meet him in half an hour in one of the little used corridors.

Jones was waiting when McKernan arrived. The corridor was cold and the director was beating his arms against his sides to keep warm. McKernan was dressed more warmly, but that wasn't what caused him to ignore the cold. He could tell that the other man had something to tell him, and that it was important. For the moment McKernan forgot about Helga.

"I haven't finished checking yet, that would take weeks. But I've turned up some discrepancies, and they're in the area that you asked about. A number of claim applications are missing. Some assay samples and reports, too. It may be coincidence, but one of the missing applications is for a man named Morrison, the one that was found shot out on his claim?"

McKernan's blood suddenly flowed hot as he stiffened. This might be the break that he was looking for. "What can you tell me about the claim."

"Quite a bit, actually. I handled it, myself. When he brought in the assay I didn't believe it at first. The sample was unbelievably rich. It looked like an obvious salting, but it wasn't. The man had struck an almost incredible deposit. Gold, silver, a dozen rare earths and commercial semiconductors all at very high concentrations. And it's so rich it hardly has to be smelted to separate them all. I don't know how big the deposit is, Morrison was pretty cagey about that, but even a few hundred tons of the same quality as the sample would make it the biggest find on Mars."

"Are you sure it was natural?" McKernan asked. "It sounds almost too good to be true."

"Oh, it was natural, but it took me a while to figure out how it could occur. There are still a lot of things that we don't know about the mineralogy of Mars. There are a lot of differences between the past history of Mars and the earth. Anyway, Morrison's claim is in one of those regions that looked so much like water erosion features in the early Mariner photos."

"Yeah, I know. I was out there to recover the body. It's like the bed of a dried up river."

"Exactly. Well, at some point in the past large parts of the Martian soil liquefied and flowed just like water to produce those channels. There actually is quite a bit of water tied up in the soil in the form of ice. It wouldn't take a large rise in temperature to melt that ice causing all the soil to turn to mud."

"As the mud flowed down the channels caused by erosion, the heaviest particles would drop out first. It's a familiar enough phenomenon. The deposits left behind are called placer deposits, and they are well known on earth. It was a placer deposit that caused the gold rush of 1849 in California. That's part of the story."

"As to the rest of it, that's more peculiar to Mars. The original source of the minerals that ended up in the deposit were volcanic in origin. Olympus Mons itself is a volcano of tremendous proportion, and the region has been the sight of a lot of volcanic activity. As magma cools, different minerals crystallize out at different temperatures, but because of differences in composition and gravity the crystallization sequence is not the same as on earth. That is why Mars is so rich in the rare earths and light metals compared to the surface of the earth."

"The placer deposits in the bed of this particular channel concentrated the particles of minerals while washing away the sand, leaving a deposit of unparalleled richness."

"Rich enough to kill for?" McKernan asked.

"Yes, maybe. With Morrison dead, the claim is free to be claimed again. If the deposit is big enough, that might be incentive enough. It's hard to believe, though, that anyone would know what Morrison had. And to plan a murder. It was planned, wasn't it?"

"Yes, it was," McKernan confirmed with a bitter note.

After a moment Jones asked, "It won't come out, about claims being stolen from the office? It would destroy public confidence in my department."

McKernan wasn't sure that was the uppermost concern on Jones's mind, but he wasn't ready to divulge anything yet. "No, I won't let it out—at least not until I catch the thief. You've been a big help to me, Jack. I'll try to keep it quiet if I can. But when I catch the thief and whoever killed Morrison, I'm not sure that I can keep it from coming out. There's bound to be some sort of an investigation by the Authority Council."

Jones nodded. "I'd best be getting back before my absence attracts too much attention.

It was all beginning to fit together in McKernan's mind. The break in at the Claims office was tied in with Morrison. The claim itself was valuable enough to kill for if he could take Jones's word for it, providing at least one link in the chain of circumstances surrounding the murder.   There were other links, or possible links, at least. Svenson and Fokuda had a claim in the same general area as Morrison's had been. The incident in Thelma's might have been more than just a bar fight. Perhaps the intent had been to put the two prospectors out of action as well.

As he walked back to the office, something was plaguing McKernan, a bit of lost data just on the edge of remembrance. He knew it was important, if only he could remember what it was.   There were too many things happening out past Olympus Mons for them all to be coincidences. First Morrison, then the two prospectors and the missing papers. But had Morrison been the first?

The missing datum suddenly came back to him. It had been something that the Anglo Martian mechanic had said when he and Helga had flown out to get Morrison's body, something about Nelson crashing out that way while doing a survey for the Arabian conglomerate that he worked for. He had known Nelson, not well, but well enough to know that he was not a careless pilot. At the time of the accident there had been no reason to suspect foul play. But now he suspected anything that had to do with the area past Olympus Mons.

Gaeretts could see that McKernan was on to something when he got back to the office. Even Ferris caught the edge of excitement. "Did something break on the Morrison case?" the younger man asked.

"Possibly, just possibly," McKernan said with a calmness that he didn't feel. "Gaeretts, do you remember when Nelson crashed last month? I want you to get the report on that. Check out all the details. If you have to, fly out to the wreckage and inspect it yourself. In fact, you'd better count on that. Call around and see if there is a free plane."

"What am I looking for?" Gaeretts asked.

"The crash might not have been an accident. I want to know one way or another."

"Are you thinking that the same one who killed Morrison might have killed Nelson?"

"It's a possibility we can't overlook now. It may be just a coincidence, but two deaths in the same part of Mars within a month is enough reason to investigate." McKernan thought for a moment about filling Gaeretts in on his suspicions, but he thought better of the idea. He'd wait until the constable got back with some positive information. He didn't want to color Gaerett's investigation with his own suspicions.

"Keep it quiet, too," he added. "If anyone asks, it's a routine check for the Authority's Safety Commission. I don't want to start a panic by letting the idea get out that there's some kind of homicidal maniac running loose."

"Okay. I'll keep it quiet. Is it important enough to fly out there today? I probably won't be able to get back before dark."

"Yes, it's important. If you can get a plane you can still land in the area before sunset and camp out overnight in the plane. It's going to take a lot of time to sift through the wreckage and I want you back some time tomorrow."

Gaeretts nodded. McKernan didn't like the idea of losing Gaeretts at a time when the case might be breaking, but he was the only man that he could count on to spot what he was looking for. He'd have to make do with Ferris and Kaminski in the mean time.

He was about to go into his office and finish his paperwork when Ferris said sheepishly, "Inspector, I almost forgot. Mr. McAndrews called and asked if you could meet him for lunch at the Mars Club."

Damn, thought McKernan, as if he didn't have enough things to worry about. It couldn't be a casual invitation, not to the Mars Club and not by McAndrews. But the invitation had the ring of a summons about it, and McAndrews was one of the few people that he could count on if Powell tried to make trouble for him.

11

The exterior of the Mars Club was anything but prepossessing, an airlock door set in the fused silica bricks with a sign fifteen centimeters on a side with the two words, "Mars Club" engraved in the steel. Inside, however, was the retreat of those people who ran the corporations on Mars, and only the biggest of those. In effect, it served as an informal governing body for the corporations on Mars, though ostensibly it was a recreation hall for the executives who were members. More disputes between corporations were resolved behind the plain door of the club than were handled by the Authority's Office of Arbitration.

McKernan had never been inside before, one of the few places on Mars that he hadn't been. There was a small buzzer next to the door. He pushed it and a moment later the door swung open to admit him. To his surprise, he was met by McAndrews, himself. He had half expected a servant in full livery to greet him with a request to use the servants entrance if there were such a thing.

As he followed McAndrews, he looked around. The place was furnished simply, but then the members of the Mars Club had enough power to be able to dispense with the outward show of it in private. It looked comfortable, but not gaudy. One wall was given over to CRT information displays of things like the stock markets and weather conditions around Mars.

McAndrews escorted him to a room in the rear of the club. Lunch, if he was going to get any, consisted of a plate of sandwiches in the center of the table that dominated the room. Around the table were seated a dozen men that he recognized.   He should; between them they ran three quarters of the mining on Mars.   There was even a representative of The Chinese People's Martian Cooperative looking every bit the equal of his capitalistic colleagues.

"Sit down please, Erik," McAndrews said, pointing to a vacant seat opposite his own.   Otis McAndrew was the Resident Manager for Anglo Martian Mining.   He had been on Mars longer than anyone at the table, nearly fifteen years, and often served as the spokesman for the corporations when they wanted to speak with one voice. He was an Englishman of the type that should have died out with the World Wars, but somehow his breed had survived. Even on Mars he wore his school's tie and always dressed impeccably.   He had a tendency to be stuffy and a bit pompous at times, but he was uncompromisingly honest. McKernan liked him.   He also respected him.   McAndrews hadn't lasted fifteen years as resident of a major corporation without being more than competent. McAndrews knew Mars and he knew mining.   He also had a reputation for fair mindedness and impartiality that made him desirable as a mediator and leader.   That and the fact that the Arabs and Japanese found him more acceptable than an American as their spokesman.

"Would you like some wine?" McAndrews asked.

"You didn't ask me down here just for lunch," McKernan said quietly as he accepted the glass.   Not with the managers of companies like BP, Siemens from Europe, Anaconda, 3M, and Texas Semiconductor from the U.S., Marabco, the company Nelson had flown for, or the representatives of the Matsushita Mitsubishi combine and the Chinese cooperative there.

"You're right," McAndrews said politely.   "There's something we want to talk to you about, but we thought it better for all concerned if our discussion remained informal and private." That was the old boy's way of saying that they didn't want to give the impression that they were interfering in Authority business, even if they were. McKernan finished cataloging the people at the table. The only significant omissions were the manager of United Semi and the Russian's man. The soviets had been late comers to Mars and they had never forgiven the others for stealing the march on them. As for United Semi, it was probably just as well. McKernan had been rubbing them the wrong way of late.

"It's about this Morrison business, McKernan. We want to know what you've done about it," one of the Americans said bluntly. "We've heard enough to know that it's more than a simple murder. We want it solved, and solved soon."

"Murder is never simple," McKernan said icily. "As to solving it, the body was discovered only a few days ago. The murderer has had at least that long to cover his tracks. An investigation like this takes time, and neither the corporations or the Authority are overly generous when it comes to staffing my department."

"Erik," McAndrews said moderately, "no one is suggesting that you aren't doing your best. We all know you and your reputation too well for that. But this murder has got us worried. The corporations—and I include our colleagues from the People's Cooperative in that because they stand to lose with the rest of us—the corporations are treading on dangerous grounds on Mars. We are here only at the sufferance of the Authority and the UN, and I have no need to remind you how political the latter is. There are a lot of the underdeveloped nations that resent our presence and the profits we make. They can use this murder as ammunition for limiting or expelling us, especially if the murderer isn't found and brought to justice. We all stand to lose a lot if that happens. We know that you are understaffed. Part of the purpose of this gathering is to offer you any help that we can in solving this crime. I am prepared to put all the resources of Anglo Martian at your disposal, unofficially, of course, and I'm sure that everyone else at this table is willing to make a similar commitment."

McKernan was somewhat mollified. McAndrews had put their position in the most careful wording. If the corporations were found intervening in Authority business it would be a powerful argument for their expulsion from Mars. However, their willing cooperation could make things easier.

"Do you have any leads, Inspector McKernan?" Kurosawa asked.

"If you mean do I have a suspect, no," McKernan answered. "But I think that I have a reasonable idea of the motive. With that I think that I can crack this case, but it's far from being solved."

"Would you care to enlighten us as to the motive?"

"I'd rather not, other than to say it has something to do with Morrison's claim. You realize that it's possible that one of you is involved in this crime."

"I think that you had better explain that," McAndrews said calmly before any of the others had a chance to interrupt.

"The man was a skilled assassin," McKernan said. "He knew what he was doing, and he was operating with complete knowledge of Morrison's movement. I doubt that he was working alone. There's also the matter of the weapon. Assuming it wasn't manufactured here on Mars, which I think is highly unlikely, it was smuggled from earth. The corporations between them control most of the ships traveling between earth and Mars. We have at least one man working on earth to get the gun on the ship, probably another on Mars other than the killer to receive it. That's getting to be rather a large conspiracy to keep concealed within a company. I have reason to believe that even more people might be involved. It would be a lot easier to arrange matters if someone high up in the corporate structure were involved."

"You don't have any proof of this, do you? As to which corporation, I mean."

"No, not yet. But if I'm right about the motive, I think only a corporation would have the resources to take advantage of it. It's too big for a small group to handle."

A Frenchman from CIE said, "It's utterly fantastic. What's to be gained by it all? Surely none of us could be involved?"

"Someone went to a lot of trouble getting some professionals to Mars. Professionals without a record or they'd never have gotten past the Authority. That means organization and money. Who else but a corporation has that?"

There was an uneasy shuffling of chairs as the impact of what he was saying sank in. The CPMC man asked, "What about the Russians? Could it be them?"

"That's a possibility, but I think a remote one. First, they haven't any operations in the area around Morrison's claim. Also, everyone is so suspicious of them that I don't think they could get away with anything. I'm not ignoring that possibility, but my instincts and the evidence point against it."

"I think that the inspector is right," McAndrews said. "Now is not the time for speculation. If what he says is true, that a conspiracy is involved, then I think it is more important than ever that this matter be cleared up as soon as possible. Erik, is there anything that we can do to help?"

"There is some information that I could use. First, Mr. Bourgabi. A Marabco flight crashed a month ago in the same general area as Morrison's claim. I'd appreciate any information you might have on that flight and other flights you've had in that area. I've got a man checking it now, but there is a lot of ground to be covered and I don't have the manpower."

"Second, I'd like a list of all personnel in that area before and after the murder. It's possible that they may have seen something that could prove helpful. Also, any reports of unusual activity in that area within the last few months."

"I don't know if any of us can be of much help there," the man from Texas Semi drawled. "The only one with much of an operation in that area is United."

"He's right," Bourgabi added, "Mars is a big planet. My company had only started to explore that area when Nelson crashed. Unfortunately that has curtailed our efforts while we await a new plane from earth."

There was a murmur around the table as one by one they all denied having operations in that specific area. McKernan had no reason to disbelieve them. "What about United Semi? Was their man invited to lunch today?"

"Yes, he was," McAndrews confirmed. "He said that he had another engagement, and that he thought we were all getting worked up over nothing. I didn't think anything of it at the time. United Semiconductor has often played the maverick as I'm sure you know. We aren't really on the best of terms. But I find it hard to believe that they would go so far as murder."

"As you said, now is not the time for speculation. For the moment I think it best it you all watch each other very closely," McKernan said as he got up from the table. "I thank you gentlemen for the lunch, but now it's time I got back to work."

Gaeretts had already taken off when McKernan got back to the office. The constable had taken the plane of one of the American companies out to the crash site. More than ever, McKernan was convinced that he would find evidence of sabotage if that evidence hadn't been destroyed in the crash. He hoped it hadn't. He needed the proof.

A lot had happened in the last twenty four hours. He needed time to put it all together, to sort out the details. Shoving back the papers on his desk, he put his feet up and ran through what he knew.

The best bet was that United Semi or someone high up in that organization had pulled the strings. The corporation was already working in the area. More than likely they knew about Morrison's find, about the geology that must underlie that whole valley.   Maybe they had just gotten greedy and had wanted it all for themselves. Or maybe they had just wanted to keep it quiet until they had it all staked out. If word of Morrison's strike had gotten out, it would have started a rush that would have made the Klondike and 1849 look pale by comparison.   Earth needed those minerals.   The price edged up a little every years, but despite that, the demand grew.

With the help of insiders it would have been easy enough to smuggle in the gun that had killed Morrison. The Authority didn't have much in the way of customs. What there was, was limited to the weekly passenger ships. The corporation ships were left alone. It was another case of not enough men or money. It had always been in the interest of the corporations to keep out drugs and weapons; they were bad for business. Therefore they had been left to police themselves. That was before one of the corporations had made murder their business.

McKernan wondered if he had made a mistake in having Penderkarass shipped back to earth. He was the only really likely suspect that had turned up so far, and if the corporation was behind him, his alibi might not be as airtight as he had thought. Unfortunately, it was too late to do anything about it. The Authority didn't have any extradition treaties. It occurred to him that the evidence might be on its way back to earth as well, or at least the weapon.

If that was the case, assuming Penderkarass had been the murderer, all that he could do was try and tie down the loose ends. The chances were that one or more of the people involved were still on Mars. If he could get enough proof he might be able to get the Authority Council to revoke United Semi's license, though the chances were that the corporation had covered itself and the most he would get would be a scapegoat.

The more McKernan thought about it the more it began to look as though he had blown it. His own eagerness had cost him Penderkarass. He wanted the man who had pulled the trigger, the man who had sat up on the cliff and gunned down Morrison in cold blood. Without him, he doubted that he'd ever get all the way to the top. With his evidence flown he might be lucky to get anyone at all. It wasn't very satisfying.

The inspector felt the need for a drink. Silently he headed for Finnegan's.

12

An insistent sound in the dark woke him, an angry buzz that echoed through the empty space of the hut. It took precious moments for McKernan to recognize it for what it was. He had gotten drunk at Finnegan's, though three years of habit had kept him from getting as drunk as he would have liked. Now as he reached for the portable phone next to his bed, his head was still a little loggy from the alcohol.

Thumbing the transmit switch he said, "McKernan here. Whoever this is you had better have a good reason for waking me."

He waited for the reply which was delayed the several seconds that indicated the call was being relayed through the communication satellites that circled Mars. "Erik? This is Helga. Listen, I don't have much time. I've seen one of the men that you arrested at Thelma's, the one that came at you with the bottle."

"It can't be him," McKernan protested. "He was sent packing back to earth."

"I know. That's why I called. I'm sure that it's him. I don't forget faces. Besides, his arm was in a sling, the one that you broke."

"Look, where are you?"

"I'm still out at United Semi's Camp # 3."

Damn, McKernan thought. Of all the places for her to be. He tried to think for a moment, trying to remember if there was anyplace nearby where she might seek safety. There wasn't any. That part of Mars was a very lonely place.

"Okay. Get off the air as soon as possible, and if you can get out of that camp without attracting attention, do it. I'll be out there as soon as I can make it. Be careful."

He keyed the receive switch again but there was no answer. The channel had gone dead. For a moment he considered trying to raise her again, but thought better of it. If she had had to get off the transmitter in a hurry, calling back would only arouse suspicions. It was still possible that Penderkarass and whoever was behind him might still be unaware of Helga's call. He didn't want to think about what would happen if they had caught her while she had been talking.

He sat on the edge of the cot trying to collect his thoughts. The clock next to the bed read 0030, an hour past midnight. Camp #3 was a couple of time zones behind. It would be 2207 there, a few minutes after ten in the evening. Not too late. If Helga had been caught, she might still be able to make a plausible excuse.

But that wasn't something that he could count on. He had to get out there as soon as possible, both to protect Helga and to get Penderkarass. He wasn't going to let him get away this time.

He realized that he was very cold. He had been sitting naked and the temperature was low, about five degrees Celsius. He could see his breath in the faint illumination of the clock. He didn't like that. It probably meant that the weather was changing, and on Mars that was always a bad sign. If he didn't get going soon, he might never get into the air. Storms like that weren't impossible. He remembered that on one of the early Mariner flights the planet had been shrouded for weeks in a blanket of dust that had blown all the way around the planet.

The thought sobered him. He couldn't go rushing off without making contingency plans. The nearest help that he could count on was Konstantin at New Klondike. The only problem was that he didn't have any air transport. Camp #3 was at least fifteen hours away by buggy, even at a top speed of forty kilometers per hour. And that was if Konstantin wasn't out doing his rounds.

He made the call anyway, routing his call through the Authority station and using a private frequency and a scrambler. Konstantin wasn't happy about the idea of driving across six hundred kilometers in the dark, but he didn't bitch when he heard the reason. He knew a couple of miners that he could trust as deputies as well. They had been friends of Morrison's.

He cursed himself again for sending off Gaeretts. He hadn't had any choice at the time, but now he needed him. If it came to trouble he wasn't sure that he could trust either Kaminski or Ferris in a fire fight. He couldn't leave the city without some sort of security, anyhow.

Gaeretts wasn't too far from the camp, maybe three hundred kilos, and he had a plane as well. But it was dark on that part of Mars, and Gaeretts wasn't that good of a pilot, not good enough to take off and land on unlighted terrain, especially when he might run into hostile fire at the other end. He'd have to wait until daybreak, but then he'd be able to make it in half an hour.

Gaeretts wasn't a good enough pilot, but he was. He thought about waiting until morning and flying in with Gaeretts, but he couldn't afford the time. Not if they had Helga. If he landed in the middle of the night there was a good chance that he might be able to surprise them. He'd better, or the odds would be pretty long on the other end.

To his knowledge, there was only one plane in town. There had been only five since Nelson had crashed, so it hadn't been hard to keep track. Gaeretts had one, Texas Semi's. United Semi had their own, probably out at Camp

#3.   Matsushita Mitsubishi's had been stripped for maintenance when he had flown out with Helga. The other was on the far side of the planet. That left Anglo Martian's.

He punched McAndrews number into the phone and waited for the answer. The resident himself answered, which was surprising considering the hour.

"Otis, this is McKernan. I've got a favor to ask of you."

A British accent answered sleepily from the instrument, "Are you aware of what the time is, Erik?"

"Yes, I know. But this is important. I think that I've found Morrison's killer, but I need a plane to go after him."

The phone was silent for a moment, but when McAndrews replied he was no longer sleepy. "Good work, Erik. I'll call the mechanic and have the plane ready for you at dawn."

"I need it now. I can't wait," McKernan said impatiently. "There is an innocent life at stake, Helga Olafson, the correspondent. I think she may have been discovered giving me the information about the murderer."

"I'm sorry, Erik," McAndrews said sympathetically. Gossip travels fast on Mars, McKernan reflected cynically. "But you can't be serious about going out there now. It's in the middle of the night. It will be dark for another nine hours at Camp #3. That is where you're going, isn't it?"

"Yes it is. Look, I need that plane of yours. I'll commandeer it if you won't give it to me."

"I can't allow it, Erik. You'll get yourself killed, and we can't afford that. Not now."

"I'm a good pilot, Otis. I flew night missions all the time in Burma. Seventy four of them. Your plane isn't that different from a Harrier."

"It's against my better judgment, but I'll have the plane standing by."

"Good. I'll be ready in about half an hour. And thanks."

"Just don't get yourself killed. Is there anything else you need? Some men to back you up?"

"I'd rather not risk anybody's life but my own. I've got Gaeretts and Konstantin coming to help." He didn't add that it would be hours before they could make it, days in the case of Konstantin. "You might watch Powell for me."

"The governor?" McAndrews asked incredulously.

"I don't have any proof, but he's in close with United Semi. I don't want to have to worry about my back."

"I understand. I'll call the mechanic now. Good luck, Erik."

The phone went dead. He tried to reach Gaeretts, but with no success. He was probably asleep. It was just as well. If he knew what was up he'd probably try to rush in and help, and as likely add his wreckage to that of Nelson's."

McKernan realized that he still hadn't dressed. He did so hurriedly, pulling on insulated underwear and a jumpsuit. He might be out on the surface for a long time, and it would be best if he dressed for it. He stashed his automatic in his shoulder holster and added the usual collection of knives. He hoped that he wouldn't have to use any of them, but he wasn't optimistic.

He was hungry, but he didn't have time. He could catch some coffee at the office and eat concentrates on the plane. Not satisfying, but it would have to do.

Kaminski was at the office when he went to pick up his surface suit. He explained the situation and left orders for Kaminski to call Gaeretts every half hour until he reached him. He was starting to worry about him, but put it out of his mind. He had enough to think about.

He checked out two weapons from the armory, the battered AR 16 and a pump action twelve gauge with a sawed off barrel. The latter didn't have much of a range, but its intimidation potential to men dressed in pressure suits was enormous. One pellet through the fabric of a suit was enough to give a man better things to do than shoot back. He stuffed a couple of extra clips in the pockets of his surface suit and a dozen rounds for the scatter gun. If he needed more than that he was going to be in big trouble.

He was about to lock the cabinet when his eye was caught by a long barreled .44 magnum revolver and holster sitting in the bottom. To his knowledge it had never been fired, but he knew that Ferris kept all the guns cleaned and in working order. In the low pressure and gravity of Mars one of those bullets would carry for kilometers and still have stopping power. For the hell of it he threw the belt over his shoulder. He rummaged around for a box of ammunition, but there were only the twelve cartridges in the belt.

Kaminski looked at him oddly as he gathered up all the hardware. "Going to start a war?"

"I'm going to stop one," McKernan said tersely.

"Are you sure you don't need help? Ferris or I could go with you."

"No, somebody has got to hold the fort. Besides, I want you to watch the spaceport. I don't want anyone from United Semi leaving until you hear different from me. I don't want anyone else going out to Camp #3, either. Understand?"

Kaminski nodded.

"Good. If you don't hear from me by ten, Gaeretts is in charge. If you don't hear from him, you're in charge. It'll be time to come running. And come loaded. You'll need it. Try to get some air transport in here in the morning, just in case. If you have any trouble go through McAndrews. Don't tell Powell anything."

"I've got you, Inspector," Kaminski said. McKernan smiled. Kaminski might be a Russian appointee, but his loyalties were to the Authority and Mars. The Russian held out his hand. McKernan shook it and then was off.

When he left the lock the wind was blowing. He could hear the fine scratch of dust being blown against his helmet. That wasn't good. So far it was only the little stuff, microscopic bits of debris, and visibility hadn't been affected much, but if the winds picked up, as they gave every indication of doing, it would be hell on the surface and worse aloft. It had been known to blow higher than Olympus Mons forty kilometers up. Wind velocities might well reach three hundred kilometers per hour. Not a pleasant prospect for the pilot of one of the fragile Marsplanes.

The Anglo Martian mechanic was there to meet him, inspecting the landing skids of the plane. Behind the faceplate of his helmet he looked sleepy.

"Is she ready to go, Arthur?" McKernan asked.

"That she is, Inspector. though I wish you had given me more time to go over her." The voice was even more heavily accented than usual and was hard to understand over the radio.

"I don't have the time."

"I figured as much, you leavin' off in the middle of night." The mechanic reached into one of the pockets of his surface suit and pulled out a packet of papers. "I stopped by the weather service and got the reports for the next twenty four hours. It's not a good night to be flying and it's going to get worse. I doubt if anything will be going up after noon."

"I'd better be going then," McKernan said. "And thanks for the weather reports, Arthur."

"That's all right, Inspector. Have a care, now. I'd never forgive you if you tore up old Betsy, here," he said as he patted one of the struts of the landing gear.

He helped McKernan with his gear, handing the weapons up without comment. McKernan buttoned up the hatch behind him and then went up into the cockpit. Arthur waved to him from outside and then went to turn on the lights for the field.

McKernan was halfway through the preflight check when they came on, a string of hundred thousand candlepower lamps running in a line parallel to the hangars. There was a thin haze almost like fog lit up in the beams of the landing lights. It wasn't fog, but dust. It was probably an illusion of the lights, but McKernan thought that the dust looked thicker than it had earlier. If the wind was rising that fast he might be in trouble.

The quicker up, the quicker he would be down. He lit the main engines and then the thrusters. The ship pirouetted uneasily in the wind as he swung her nose into it and towards the west. Hovering, the ship was awkward, the great expanse of the wings vibrating in the wind. He didn't think about what it would be like landing on a darkened field. Instead, he opened the throttles and pulled up on the nose to gain some altitude.

13

Flying through the Martian night provided an eerie sensation, much stranger than it had ever been over Burma. McKernan was flying over uninhabited territory, and there were no lights on the surface that raced by a few hundred meters below. There wasn't any moonlight, either. Neither of Mars's tiny satellites was big enough to give off any useable illumination even if they had been above the horizon.

Not that McKernan was in any danger. The plane had a full complement of instruments and radar. As long as he paid attention, he wouldn't run into anything like the side of a mountain, and with only five planes on the planet, he wasn't likely to have a midair collision. But knowledge of those facts didn't help his nerves. He knew that he hadn't had enough sleep, and that he had drunk too much at Finnegan's to be racing through the night to confront an unknown number of murderers. It wasn't a circumstance to settle one's mind.

He found himself thinking back nine years to the times he had flown another type of plane through other nights. He had been flying a fighter bomber over the jungles of Burma. He had rarely seen his targets then; they had all been pinpointed by a laser beam from an unseen spotter. He had known, though, that death awaited him in the form of a SAM fired by an infiltrator in black pajamas. He had been lucky, he had flown his seventy four missions without a scratch, but death had waited for him just the same.

He had never gotten used to it. He wasn't any better prepared for it now. Once he got into action it had always been okay. Then he had had something to do. But flying through the dark before reaching his target, that gave him time to think. He hadn't really supported the war, not once he had gotten over there, but the draft hadn't left him with many choices, and the veteran's benefits when he had gotten out had meant the difference between a degree and the dole. He had served his hitch, but his main concern had been saving his skin.

It all came back to him, and he didn't like the feeling. He would see it through, though, just as he had done then. He didn't have much choice this time, either. The job was his, and it wasn't a thing that he could give to anyone else.

He took a reading on the radar beacon to check his course. With the wind rising, he had to compensate a little, but he was still less than a kilometer off. Room enough on Mars. He wasn't sure whether it was just the instrument lights reflecting off the inside of the cockpit bubble or not, but he was having a hard time seeing the stars. If there was that much dust in the atmosphere already, it was going to be hell by morning; no flying, instruments or not. That ruled out much chance of help except for Konstantin. It might be a week until the dust settled out of the atmosphere. Or a month.

It was time that he made some plans. He didn't like the idea of just dropping in on the camp. It gave them too much of a chance to pull something. He didn't want to end up like Nelson. On the other hand, they probably didn't have much in the way of radar at Camp #3, and with the storm he'd be hard to spot. If he could find a flat spot within a kilometer or so he could land and they'd never know it. That way he could walk in quietly.

He checked the map and there was such a place, though it was smaller than he would have liked, and the terrain symbol indicated the presence of craters up to several meters in diameter. Old Arthur would never forgive him if he dropped the plane into one of those. It was only a kilometer from the camp over a shallow rise. That would shield the plane from sight if anybody should happen to peek out.

He took another fix on the radar beacon to make sure that he wasn't drifting with the wind. The indicator said that it was blowing at a hundred and eleven meters per second at his altitude, though near the ground that velocity would die off. It had better, as that was close to two hundred and fifty kilometers per hour.

McKernan switched off the running lights. He was getting close enough to be spotted. In fact, he could see the lights of the compound though they were periodically obscured by the dust. He pointed the plane south a couple of degrees and began his descent. He was going to waste a lot of fuel on the landing, but he didn't really care. This was one time when he didn't want to pile up.

He cut the throttles and came in slowly on the down thrusters until he was almost hovering. The altimeter display was bouncing digits as he passed over irregularities on the surface twenty meters below. He didn't want to risk the landing lights so he played it by feel, checking his air speed and then coming down ever so gently on his thrusters.

He touched and cut the engines immediately. It was a soft enough landing even if it did leave him with the nose fifteen degrees up in the air and a with list to starboard. It wasn't bad for being blind. He sat back for a moment to collect himself and turned the receiver to the channel used for communications between suits. He couldn't pick up anything. If they had heard him they weren't announcing the fact.

He checked his watch. By local time it was 2430, a few minutes before midnight. The witching hour, he thought wryly. Well, there were going to be some surprises that night. he began to check his equipment, making sure that he was ready for the surface.

He loaded the guns, making sure that he had the extra ammo where he could reach it. There was nothing worse than having something that you needed in a pocket inside your surface suit where you couldn't get at it. McKernan was almost embarrassed by the arsenal that he was carrying. If he was wrong, he was going to look awfully foolish. He didn't think that he was wrong, though.

Once outside, he staked down the plane thoroughly. The wings were flapping up and down until he tied down the skids at their tips. If the wind really picked up, the plane might flip over. He had landed pointing into the wind. He hoped that the direction wouldn't change much. It probably wouldn't. The big storms blew clear around the planet chasing their tails.

He could hear the wind shriek through his helmet. It was a strange sound, for normally the air was too thin to produce much noise. When he turned on his helmet light the air was thick with dust, almost red in color. It reminded him of the air back home in Los Angeles.

There weren't any stars visible to guide himself by, and the rise was still between himself and the camp. Fortunately, he had an inertial compass to steer by. He needed it. Fifty paces from the plane he lost sight of it in the dark. As he stood trying to find it he noted that his prints were already filling up with windblown dust. Normally, prints could remain visible for weeks, even months.   Now he doubted that there was a trail that he could follow back to the plane.

The rise wasn't much. He could hardly tell that he was walking up hill. He was over the top before he knew it. Then he saw the lights of the camp about ten degrees off from where he had expected them. He flicked off his own helmet light and crouched low to the ground, but he didn't see anyone out and watching him. That didn't surprise him. He wouldn't go out on a night like that, himself, unless he had to.

He tried to orient himself. He had only been to Camp #3 twice, the last time over six months earlier. There had been some new construction since then, but the main plan of the camp hadn't changed much.   The VIP building and headquarters were in the middle connected to the barracks and the shops by tunnels that came off each end. Behind, in another row, were the warehouses and vehicle parks, and lost in the dust were the smelters.   It was a fair sized operation with, perhaps, two hundred and fifty men there at a time and another eighty man shift taking a week of R&R in New Klondike or Mars City.   New Klondike was more likely. It was closer.

Helga was probably in the VIP building.   At least he hoped that she was. Otherwise the camp was a big place to search without being seen.   He'd save Penderkarass for later. He checked his guns again and then slung the carbine over his shoulder. The scatter gun he kept in his hand.

————————

It was easy crossing the open space that stretched between the rise and the buildings of the camp. Except for himself and the swirl of windblown dust, there was no sign of movement. There was an airlock set in the side of the big pressurized half cylinder that served as the headquarters of the camp. McKernan reached it and crouched by the wall for a moment as he caught his breath.

There was no lock on the airlock. No reason for one. The owner's hadn't expected intruders to come unannounced from the Martian outback. McKernan spun the wheel that opened it and set the controls on cycle. He waited impatiently while the chamber was purged and pressure built up again to a breathable level.

Inside there was a reception area facing the lock. A man sat there manning a console that contained readouts on the power and life support systems of the camp. He looked surprised when McKernan walked through the lock, more surprised yet when he saw the shotgun that the lawman held in his hands.

"I'm Inspector McKernan of Authority Security," he said, carefully pointing the shotgun at the floor, but ready to bring it into play in a hurry.

The man seemed struck dumb, unable to believe what was happening. McKernan reached into a pocket and brought out a plastic coated ID with his picture. "This will prove who I am. Now I want you to get up and stand away from the console. Move carefully so that I can see your hands." He gestured with the gun for effect.

"Hadn't I better get the supervisor, Inspector?" the man asked.

"There will be time for that later. Right now do you know which room Helga Olafson is using?" The man nodded. "Okay. Lead me to it, and if we meet anybody, let me do the talking."

The man led him down a corridor lined with doors at regular intervals. There were numbers on the doors, and in some cases, names. They stopped before one without a name. McKernan opened it without knocking. He didn't like what he saw. The room had been searched, thoroughly, but not neatly. A couple of rolls of film lay exposed on the bed along with much of Helga's camera equipment. He poked through the tiny closet with the shotgun, but her surface suit was missing.

"All right, where is she?" McKernan asked icily.

"I don't know. Honest. I just take care of the life support equipment. I've hardly even seen the woman since she got here." The man eyed the end of the shotgun nervously as if he were afraid it might go off.

"Where's the radio room?" McKernan followed as the attendant showed him the way. The room was locked, but the door wasn't heavy. McKernan kicked his way through the plastic. There wasn't anyone inside there, either. He noticed that the front panel of the transmitter had been opened and the crystals removed. Without the crystals, the set was effectively sabotaged, cutting the camp off from the outside world.

"I'm starting to lose my patience. Maybe we ought to see that supervisor now." The attendant looked relieved. He had been wondering how long the inspector's temper would keep his finger away from the trigger on the shotgun.

McKernan didn't knock at the supervisor's door, either. He had to prod the man awake with the barrel of the shotgun. The supervisor sputtered awake, but his protest stopped when he saw the gun pointed at him.

"What's the meaning of this, McKernan?" he asked, pulling together what little dignity he had left. "You can't come barging in here like this without a warrant."

"This isn't Earth, and the Authority Charter and the license you operate under give me exactly that right. It doesn't matter, though. I have reason to believe that a serious crime has been committed tonight, and as you see,

I'm the man holding the gun. Now I suggest that you cooperate with me, if only for the latter reason."

"What do you want? I don't know what you're talking about."

"For starters, where is Helga Olafson? She isn't in her room, and it's been ransacked. Also, you might explain to me why your transmitter has been sabotaged, and why a man who was supposed to have been expelled from Mars several days ago was seen in this camp a few hours ago."

The supervisor looked puzzled. McKernan couldn't be sure, but the reaction seemed genuine. He wasn't that surprised. There were probably only a handful of people in United Semi that were directly involved. Camp #3 was a big place, and things could easily have been concealed from the supervisor.

"I don't know what you mean by any of this, but I assure you that I haven't had any part in it. If, as you claim, some crime has occurred, I'm as eager to get to the bottom of it as you are, Inspector."

McKernan thought for a moment. The man was probably telling the truth, and he wasn't getting anyplace on his own. It would take him hours to search the camp on his own, and he wouldn't be able to do it without giving himself away to Penderkarass and his accomplices.

"For the moment I'm willing to accept your word for that. You'd better not be lying, though. I'm going to need your help. Do you know a man named Penderkarass?"

The supervisor slumped back, happy that McKernan was talking reasonably. "Yes, he's on one of our exploration teams. He should be in camp now. Why?"

"I want to see him. He's wanted for murder. Send your man here after him and have him brought here. And he better not tip Penderkarass off or I'll have you both as accessories to murder."

The attendant went off to the barracks. McKernan let the supervisor get dressed, though the man appeared nervous at having to do it under the lawman's watchful eye. While they waited, they talked, and the supervisor confirmed the fact that Penderkarass and his two buddies had been working out of Camp #3 at the time Morrison had been shot. He wasn't sure about the exact date, but somewhere around that time they had been out on a survey for a week. That was more than enough time to get to Morrison's camp and wait for him. The supervisor seemed glad to cooperate, if only to remove the shadow of guilt from himself, but his tale was cut short by the return of the attendant.

"I couldn't find Penderkarass. No one has seen him since about ten. I checked the rec room and the lounge, too, but he wasn't around. He might be in one of the other buildings, but I didn't check. You can't get to them without a surface suit."

"Did you check to see if his surface suit was missing?" McKernan asked pointedly.

From the blank expression of the night attendant he could tell that the man hadn't even thought checking. It didn't make much difference. With Helga's own suit gone, it seemed likely that she was being held in one of the outbuildings. He didn't want to think of the alternatives.

"Do either of you have any good guesses as to where they're holed up?"

The supervisor looked blank, but the other man spoke up. "They might be at the lab where exploration samples are processed. It's a small building on the edge of the camp.

The power monitors on the life support board showed that there was some activity there tonight."

McKernan looked questioningly at the supervisor. "There shouldn't be anyone working there this late," he answered, trying to sound helpful without committing himself.

"Okay, gentlemen," McKernan said nastily. "Why don't you get on your surface suits. I think that it's time for us to take a little walk."

14

Neither of them was too happy with the idea, but McKernan's gun carried a lot of weight in the final argument. They suited up reluctantly under his watchful eye. For a moment he thought about arming them, but he decided against that. They were too much of an unknown factor, especially the supervisor.

Outside, the dust storm was worse than ever. It was getting hard to see the outlines of the next row of buildings even though the camp was well lit. On earth, the wind would have produced a roar. There, it only made a thin keening that they heard through their helmets, that and a whisper of dust impacting against the fabric of their suits.

McKernan let the attendant take the lead while he held the rear with the shotgun at the ready. The building they were heading towards was a low half cylinder isolated at the end of the camp. From the main building it had been totally obscured by the dust and the night. The inspector tried to check for footprints in the sand from an earlier visit to the lab, but the storm had already erased any such sign.

The camps weather station was on top of a high pole that they passed. He could see the anemometer twirling away furiously. The windsock showed the wind to be coming from the west, the typical direction for storms at that latitude. It was shaping up to be a classic blow in the Martian tradition. It might not be as bad as the storm of Mariner 9, but nothing would be able to fly for days, possibly even weeks. With no oceans to form barriers, the storm could blow its way around the planet for a long time until it finally burnt itself out.

He wondered how Gaeretts was doing. If he had known that the storm was coming he wouldn't have sent him out. He knew that Gaeretts was too bound by his sense of duty to have turned back without getting the evidence from the site of Nelson's crash. Now he stood a good chance of being marooned until the storm died down. Fortunately, he was an old Mars hand, and he wouldn't do anything stupid. The plane would have survival gear and emergency rations. He might not be comfortable, but he wouldn't be in any real danger, not for a few weeks, at least.

McKernan's worries about Gaeretts might have distracted him. As they approached the lab he didn't notice anything unusual. Suddenly he saw a spurt of dust a few centimeters from his foot. Instinctively he dove for the ground cradling the scatter gun in his hands. The attendant followed his lead, but the supervisor was slow on the uptake. Too slow, for a moment later McKernan saw a hole blossom in the small of his back.

There wasn't any point in trying to save him, the man was dead already. The air was bitter cold, perhaps minus eighty degrees. The blood and tissue around the wound were already beginning to freeze when McKernan got to the body. Instead, the lawman sought shelter behind the corpse. Ahead of him the night man was trying to bury himself in the dust.

He tried to spot the sniper. Somebody had turned off the light above the airlock into the building shrouding the front in darkness. There was just enough light from the other buildings for him to see a lump in the shadow by one corner. He pumped two quick shots in that direction. The lump sprawled in the sand. He could see the long form of a high powered rifle laying next to the body.

The attendant looked back at him, but McKernan motioned him to stay put. He doubted that there had been just the one man. It certainly hadn't been the man who had shot Morrison who was lying in the dust. If it had been, McKernan never would have gotten off a shot. They were less than twenty meters from the lab. An easy shot for a man who could pick his target from a kilometer away.

Suddenly a stirring of dust puffs laced the sand in front of the body edging towards him. There was a peculiar quality of fantasy about them. The thin Martian air carried only a little of the sound and the dust, once thrown up fell back too slowly to seem real. He raised his head to see a man darting for the lock. He was carrying some sort of machine pistol.

McKernan fired at him, emptying the last three shells in the scatter gun as he drew a pattern across the front of the lab. He hadn't gotten a clean hit, he'd been lying too low for that, but at least a few of the pellets must have gotten him, piercing the skin of his surface suit. He'd done quite a bit of damage to the lab as well. It was hard to see in the dark, but there were three patches of discoloration in the aluminum skin. From the clouds of vapor forming, he could tell that he had pierced the inner skin. It wasn't decompressing explosively, but those inside would be scrambling to get into their surface suits.

He dropped the scatter gun as useless and reached for the pistol as he raced for the lock. He might not have killed the man, but for the moment he didn't care. He wanted to get into that building and he wanted to do it fast.

The outer door to the lock swung open easily. He got inside and pulled it shut. Unfortunately, the lock was an automatic one with a failsafe built into it. It wouldn't open until the pressure in the lock was equal to that inside the building. They'd know that he was coming through because the dogs that latched it were visible on both sides of the door.

He watched the telltale of the pressure gauge, then slanting close to the wall on the side away from the hinges he kicked the door open. Four shots from an automatic pistol splattered against the opposite wall. The sound was deafening after the silence of outside.

McKernan crouched low and sprang through the door, the big revolver ready to fire. He got off one shot rolling and then ducked behind a heavy lab table. From the glimpse he had gotten as he rolled across the floor, there were at least three men hiding behind a similar bench. The air was leaking more rapidly now that his shot had punched another hole in the skin of the building.

As he leaned against the bench, he heard the impact of a couple of shots against it. Fortunately, it was too thick for the shots to penetrate. He tried his own gun. The .44 magnum tore through the bench across from him and he heard a satisfying groan. The wood and metal didn't provide much of a barrier against the heavy revolver.

"This is McKernan. I've got you outgunned. Throw out your weapons and hold up your hands where I can see them."

"Think again, McKernan," came a voice over the suit radio. The inspector thought that he recognized the voice as Penderkarass's. "I've got your girlfriend here, and I've got a gun to her head. You fire another shot and I'll blow her head off. And she's between me and you so don't get any bright ideas about trying to get me first."

"He's telling the truth, Erik," Helga said over the radio. "I'm sorry."

"Yeah," Penderkarass said harshly. "Well she's going to be a lot sorrier if you don't stand up and drop your gun,

Inspector. You know I'll do it, too. I don't have much to lose."

McKernan didn't see much choice. He wasn't sure of where Penderkarass was behind the bench, and he wasn't going to trust himself to shoot blind hoping to miss Helga.

"I'm waiting, McKernan. And I'm getting damned impatient. I'll give you to three. One."

"Two."

McKernan stood up and laid the revolver on the table top in front of him, Across the room another figure in a surface suit stood facing him. His right arm was in a sling, but in his left hand he held a small, mean looking automatic.

"All right. Slide the gun away from you using just the little finger of your left hand. Don't try anything, either, because I'm a dead shot with either hand."

McKernan did as he was told. The automatic was only a 7mm, but the hole in the end looked big enough. He didn't have any doubts about Penderkarass's marksmanship, either.

"Okay. Now drop the carbine on the floor and kick it away from you. Grab it only by the barrel." McKernan complied. Penderkarass was coming on like a professional, but then he was. Interdicting insurgents as a ranger in Burma had been good training, he thought wryly. One survived by being careful.

Another man rose from behind the table. He was shorter than Penderkarass by quite a bit and his surface suit looked too new to have seen much use. It wasn't one of Goldschmidt's, either, but an earth made one unmodified. It was hard to tell through the visor of his suit, but he looked like the chief geologist for United Semi. That figured, McKernan thought. The man had always liked to live well, and if there was a quirk involving geology he would have been called in on it.

"I don't think Guineri is going to make it," the geologist said. "He's shot pretty badly." Guineri was the United personnel man.

"That's too bad," Penderkarass said as if it were a joke. "You're pretty good, McKernan. Not good enough, though. I assume that you got the two outside?"

"I got one for sure. The other got a few pieces of buckshot in him. He wasn't moving when I came in." McKernan didn't see any point in holding anything back. Penderkarass didn't seem the sort to hold his companions too dear. Penderkarass just smiled when he told him about the dead men.

"Okay. doc. Go over and see if he's got any more surprises hidden on him. He came in here like a walking arsenal. He's probably got a few more tricks on him."

The geologist came over and took McKernan's knife and ammo belt from him. He patted him down as well, but he didn't check too closely. He missed the pistol in the shoulder holster inside the surface suit. Not that it was going to do the lawman much good. Already the pressure was low enough that a man couldn't breathe the air. And he wasn't going to be able to crack his suit without Penderkarass noticing.

The latter tossed the geologist a piece of nylon rope. "Tie him up good. I don't want him to get loose."

The geologist did as he was told, pinning McKernan's arms behind his back. The rope bit into the insulation of the suit holding him tightly. There wasn't much hope of wriggling free.

"What are we going to do, Penderkarass?" the geologist asked. "We can't hope to hide all these bodies."

"We can and we will," Penderkarass said calmly. "The two outside aren't even supposed to be on Mars. If we dump them in the outback no one will be the wiser. Guineri can be handled in the same way. He's supposed to be on the other side of the planet at Camp #1. Eventually there might be a stink, but by then we can be safely on earth. Mars has no such thing as extradition."

"As for these two, well, McKernan probably left word that he was on his way here, so we can't hide that fact. He's probably got a plane close by, too. But I've got a plan. We take him and his girlfriend out in one of the buggies like they were trying to get somewhere, or maybe just going for a midnight drive. There's been a lot of talk about these two. We lose them and the buggy someplace in the outback. If we pick a good place it might be years before they're found, if ever. We'll be safe by then."

"There's bound to be suspicion's aroused, Penderkarass. It's too much of a coincidence. There's bound to be some sort of investigation."

"Maybe there will be, but it doesn't make any difference. If they can't find any bodies, there won't be any proof. The Authority only has so much power. They can't hold us indefinitely on suspicion. The worst that can happen is that they'll expel us, and once we're on Earth, we're home free. There's nothing they can do to us. It won't matter if they find the bodies then."

"There's one problem, Penderkarass," McKernan said, hoping to make a rift between the geologist and the killer. "One of your friends got the camp supervisor. He's lying outside with a hole in his back. That's going to be pretty hard to cover up."

"Well, he'll just have to make the trip with you and the girl. A little less romantic with a chaperone along, but I think that they'll buy it. The three of you go out in the storm on some kind of rescue mission. You get caught in it. Something goes wrong and you lose your way. Buggies have disappeared in storms before. I think that we can pull it off, especially if we have friends in high places who have to approve any report."

McKernan was sure that Powell would be only too willing to cooperate. He was glad that he hadn't mentioned the attendant. If he had any kind of brains the man was safe by now. He'd tell Konstantin what had happened when the constable finally got there.

"We'd better get moving," Penderkarass said. He yanked Helga up from behind the bench. Her hands were tied behind her, but she looked all right. There wasn't anything wrong with her suit, at least.

Penderkarass pushed her out into the middle of the room. "You take them out to one of the buggies. Use his gun to keep him under control. Don't worry about aiming it. You hit him anywhere with that cannon and he's as good as dead. I'll get the guns and clean up in here."

15

The two captives were stuffed into the back of one of the Mars buggies that stood in a line not far from the laboratory hut. Once inside, the geologist tied their feet and left. He returned several minutes later, this time bearing the body of the camp supervisor. Penderkarass was with him, but with his broken arm he did little more than hold a gun while the geologist did the work. He laid the body between Helga and McKernan on the floor of the van.

They were left alone again, presumably while the geologist and Penderkarass cleaned up the rest of the bodies. Idly McKernan wondered how they would explain the damage to the laboratory. Between the shotgun blasts and the revolver he had managed to put quite a few holes in the building.

McKernan spent the next ten minutes trying to get lose. He didn't have much luck. It would take a lot longer to break through the tough rope. He had a knife inside his suit, but like the automatic nestled under his armpit, it might as well have been a thousand kilometers away. The geologist hadn't pressurized the buggy, and even if McKernan had been able to get his suit open he would probably die before he could get at the knife.

He made an effort to raise his body and look at Helga on the other side of the supervisor's corpse. He could see the faceplate of her helmet and the face behind it. She tried to smile at him, but the effort failed. She was in an even less comfortable position than he was. He could see a bruise forming on her cheek. She hadn't been caught without a struggle. McKernan made a silent vow to kill Penderkarass slowly if he got the chance.

The geologist finally returned alone. He had the revolver stuck into the utility belt of his suit. Climbing over them, he got into the driver's seat and began the warm up check list for the buggy. McKernan could hear the hiss of air as it bled into the compartment from the storage tanks, and then the whine of the heater fan.

From where he had been dumped he couldn't see the driver's seat, but after a short interval he heard footsteps. The geologist was crouching over Helga. He turned to McKernan and removed his helmet. He had evidently done the same for Helga. The air in the vehicle was freezing but breathable.

The geologist returned to the driver's seat and the buggy began to move. Penderkarass and the bodies of his henchmen must have been put in the other buggy, McKernan thought. Their plan would be to fake an accident or disappearance of Helga, the supervisor, and himself in the one buggy while they returned in the other. It wasn't a bad plan. If it weren't for the attendant back at the camp they might even have had a chance of getting away with it.

The radio crackled to life with Penderkarass's voice. "Keep close to me, Orloff. The dust is blowing pretty thick. I don't want you to get lost on me."

"Don't worry," the geologist replied. "Let's just get this done with. I don't like murdering people in cold blood."

"It's a little late for that, isn't it?" Penderkarass asked. After that there was no more conversation.

Once they were away from the camp the going got bumpy. Lying on the floor, McKernan felt every jolt. The supervisor pressed stiffly against him, the corpse a block of ice after half an hour outside. He wondered what the body would be like when it began to thaw. He certainly wasn't a very pleasant traveling companion.

McKernan couldn't see much from the floor. He couldn't even see Helga because of the body between them. Finally, he slept because there was nothing else to do.

Sometime later McKernan woke, his back stiff and his hands and shoulders killing him from being bound behind his back. He had no idea how long he had slept, but the inside of the buggy was illuminated by weak sunlight. They had been traveling six or seven hours at the least, enough time for them to have traveled a couple of hundred kilometers. Penderkarass wasn't taking any chances on their being discovered quickly.

"You know that you aren't going to get away with this, Orloff," he said. "Things have gotten too messy. There are too many loose ends to be tied up."

"You've made things difficult for us, McKernan. I'll grant you that. But not impossible, I think. As Penderkarass explained at the camp, I think we should be able to cover our tracks well enough."

"You're a little too late for that," McKernan said. "I had some pretty good suspicions of what has been happening out here before I came out—suspicions that I confided in a couple of my men before I left. I don't think that any of you are going to get off planet before there's a full investigation. At this moment, a couple of my men are heading for Camp

#3. You won't be able to get away. You'll make it easier on yourself if you give up now and surrender to me."

"You Americans are always so optimistic. I think that you've overestimated your hand, McKernan. Besides, do you really think that Penderkarass would let me turn you loose. He's got all the guns, and he's a killer. I have no mistaken notions about my own skill in that area. No, I'm much safer going along with his plan."

The geologist wasn't about to be convinced, but he seemed to be in a mood to talk. Driving the buggy was proving to be monotonous work, and Penderkarass wasn't much of a conversationalist. McKernan saw no point in objecting. Orloff's volubility might prove valuable evidence in the unlikely event that they should survive.

"I think that you really underestimate the powers behind our little scheme, McKernan. We've bought off quite a few members of the Authority Council, not that that proved difficult. The third world types are always ready to strip the corporations of their wealth, especially if they can line their own pockets at the same time. Without hard proof, I don't think that any action will be taken. After all, Mars is a long way from earth. The lives of a few colonials more or less isn't really very important. It's money and power that matter on earth."

"We mean to have both. I'm not sure you realize what this strike that we've discovered means. You know about the strike, I assume?" Orloff didn't wait for an answer. "It's far richer than anything ever before. The only parallel that I can think of is the Namib in southern Africa. When United Semi gets control of it they'll own Mars. Refining costs will be cut in half. We'll be able to undercut everybody else on Mars, and provide all of earth's needs for the next five years. By that time, the other corporations will be off Mars and out of business. United Semi will be alone and able to dictate prices on earth. You know what control of oil did to the Arabs in the last century. Let's face it, McKernan. Technology is the only thing that holds overpopulated earth together. Without electronics, there will be chaos. Starvation, war, you name it. And we will hold the trump card."

"Do you really think that the other corporations will let you take over the most valuable tract of land on Mars?" McKernan asked.

"They will have no say in the matter. The people behind United Semi are working to get the Authority Council to grant us the claim. I told you that we had bought a good part of the council. In a few weeks that valley will be irrevocably ours. That's why we went to such lengths to keep the existence of the deposits a secret. If word got out even now, the other corporations might be able to get their fingers in the pie, or at least keep United Semi from taking control. But after the fact, I don't think so. To the nonaligned nations in the UN, their complaints will sound like so many sour grapes. The corporations are not greatly loved on much of Earth. And they are too jealous of each other to present a truly united front."

"No, Inspector, I don't think that we'll be stopped. We've planned too well since the deposits were discovered eighteen months ago. Too many people have been bought. Too many people in high places."

"Like Powell?"

"Still playing the policeman, I see," Orloff said with a laugh. "Well, maybe I had better not say any more about that."

The geologist lapsed into silence for a moment, but he seemed to have an irresistible urge to talk. "You know, it was my idea to look for alluvial deposits, an idea that my colleagues ignored, I might add. United Semi didn't think my theories were too crack brained, though. They were more than willing to take a chance and send out research teams where I directed. And the deposits were there, just where I had said they'd be."

"What do you get out of this, Orloff?" McKernan asked, hoping to irritate the geologist. "It would seem to me, that since the deposits have been discovered, your usefulness is at an end. What's to keep you friend, Penderkarass, from killing you, too."

"My death would be too much of a coincidence, I should think. Too big a risk. Besides, my demands are rather modest when one considers the scope of the profits to be made in this venture. I know that you keep a mental dossier on everyone on Mars, so I'm sure that you know I have a fondness for the pleasures life can provide. Well, I assure you, my employers are willing to provide me with ample funds to enjoy those pleasures. I shall return to earth and live quietly, but happily, and for quite some time. I am not overly greedy, as my employers realize, and unlike the villains in mystery novels, they have no plans to eliminate the underlings. I've proved my value. I might prove of value, again."

Before the argument could continue, the buggy came to a stop. "Why have we stopped?" Orloff asked into the radio.

"We've gone far enough," Penderkarass's voice came back. It's time to dump the bodies. I'll need your help to get them out of the buggy and hide them, so get over here."

"What about these two?"

"We'll take care of them later. I'd rather not shoot them, in case they are found sometime. We'll fake an accident with the buggy later. Right now let's take care of these bodies."

"All right, I'll be right over."

McKernan heard Orloff's movements as he put on his helmet. To his relief, the geologist used the airlock to exit the vehicle rather than evacuating the whole buggy. If he hadn't done that, they would have no chance at all.

16

"Helga," he called. He got no answer. The body of the supervisor was between them, so he pushed it into her to get her attention. When he called again, she responded.

"Erik, what's happening?"

"Listen. We don't have much time. Do you think that you can get my right boot off?"

"I don't see how," she replied without much interest."I've got a knife inside. I can't get at it, but if you can get it, we can cut ourselves free. If we don't, they'll kill us."

"I'll try."

McKernan could hear her struggling to move. To get at him she had to turn around and crawl over the corpse. It was a hard, painful process. There was little room to move in the buggy's cramped interior. Often she had to pause to catch her breath and twice he heard her hold back a cry of pain as the ropes bit into her.

"I can feel your boot now," she said. It had taken her half a dozen minutes to get that far. McKernan hoped that they would have time before Orloff came back. "Can you roll over on your side? I can't get at the zipper."

He complied and could feel her working at the closure on his boot. The position was awkward and she worked clumsily. Helga's task was made more difficult by the fact that the ropes binding her hands had cut off the circulation to them and made them numb.

It seemed to take forever, but he felt the boot finally slide down off his foot, and the caress of Helga's fingers on his ankle. He felt the blade slip out of its sheathe.

"Damn. I dropped it," she cried as he heard the clatter of steel on the floor of the buggy.

"Take it slow," he encouraged her." You're doing just fine. Pick up the knife and see if you can cut my hands free."

He heard her scrabbling on the floor as she sought the knife. "It's no good. I can't get to your hands. The body is in the way."

"Okay. Rest a minute," McKernan said. They were too close to give up. "Can you cut the ropes tying my legs together? If you can get that, maybe I can move into a better position." She didn't answer, but a moment later he felt her sawing at the ropes around his legs. He kept the knife sharp, and in a moment the ropes parted. His legs were numb and cramped, but he managed to raise his body into a kneeling position so that his hands were near the knife. Encouraged by her success, Helga worked on them quickly, parting the strands that held him.

Free, he cut the ropes confining Helga. She responded gratefully, sitting up and rubbing the circulation back into her hands. Working the front zipper of his suit, McKernan reached in and drew the automatic from his shoulder holster.

"Are you okay?" he asked as he worked the slide and made sure that there was a bullet in the chamber of the gun.

"Yes. A little cramped and cold, but I'm fine. I'm also hungry."

"Good. Get your helmet back on. There may be some shooting when we drive away. The buggy will hole pretty easily, and we may lose our air in a hurry."

McKernan went up front to the driver's seat and took a look at the buggy's gauges. They had plenty of fuel, enough to go a thousand kilometers or more. That was the least of their worries. He took a look around through the windshield. The other buggy was about fifteen meters away. He could hardly see it though it had its running lights on, so heavily was the sand blowing. There weren't any signs of either Penderkarass of Orloff, but if they had been more than fifty meters away, they would have been lost in the dust even with their lights on.

"Okay," he said as Helga climbed into the seat next to him. "Let's get going." Fortunately, Orloff had left the turbine idling. The machine lurched into motion as they headed away from the other vehicle. McKernan expected to hear shots at any moment, but there were none.

Their escape was anything but rapid. With poor visibility, McKernan was forced to crawl along at twenty kilometers an hour, and after he had put a kilometer between them and their captors he dropped the speed even lower. He was driving over unfamiliar terrain, and it wasn't easy going, either. Only the fact that Penderkarass was behind them with more and bigger guns kept him from stopping all together.

The first few kilometers they drove in silence, but when they had put enough distance between them so that he could breathe easier, he turned to Helga and asked, "How are you doing?"

"I'll be okay," she said. The color had come back to her face, as had a smile. "Thanks for bailing me out, Erik. I had thought that it was all over for a while there."

"We aren't out of it yet, but I think that we've got a pretty good chance, now," McKernan said as he nudged the buggy around a three meter crater. "You sure that you're all right?"

"Yes, fine. Though I could do with something to eat and some water. I haven't had anything since before supper last night."

"There should be some emergency rations in the back and a tank of water. If we're lucky, there might be something stronger to drink, too. There's usually a bottle hidden on these things somewhere."

McKernan stopped the buggy while Helga went to the back and began rummaging around in the storage compartments built into the walls. He put the time to good advantage, getting a radio fix on their position from the beacon satellites around the planet.

"Erik. What are we going to do about him?" Helga asked, pointing down at the body on the floor of the buggy.

"I'm afraid that we'll have to keep him along as evidence. It just wouldn't do to chuck him out the back, but I can tie him to the roof if it really bothers you."

"No. I guess I'm not that squeamish. It's just not pleasant riding with a corpse." She smiled up at him, ignoring the body as she stepped over it. "You were right about the bottle. I found it in with the first aid supplies."

"Not a very imaginative hiding place," was McKernan's only comment. He waited until Helga had regained her seat and then got the buggy moving again.

Helga opened a couple of ration packs and handed one to McKernan as he drove. The bar of concentrate wasn't exactly tasteless, but it did take some imagination to convince one that it was food. He chewed mechanically, his concentration centered on the terrain ahead and the swirls of dust that obscured it.

"This stuff is awful," Helga exclaimed from the seat next to him.

"Yeah, but it contains enough protein to sustain you for a couple of days at least."

"No, I mean the booze," she laughed. "Have a sip."

McKernan took the proffered bottle and downed a healthy slug. The liquor burned mercilessly on the way down and left a heavy feeling in his stomach. "Ah, yes. A local product. Aged at least a month if I'm any judge of whiskey."

"Whiskey? Is that what it's supposed to be?" Helga asked incredulously. "I would have had a hard time guessing."

"It takes time to train ones palate, but the flavor of burnt coffee grounds and charred bread crusts gives it away." After the tense time since they had been captured, they both felt the need for release, even if it meant being silly. He passed the bottle back and noted that Helga took a healthy swallow before capping it.

"What's going to happen now?" she asked more seriously. "They'll be waiting for us back at the camp, won't they?"

"I hope so," McKernan answered. I've only got this little pop gun, and they've got a couple of rifles, a machine gun, and a couple of big handguns. Penderkarass knows how to use them, too. There's not much of a match between us. I'd like to avoid a confrontation if I can. At least until I can get some reinforcements."

"Where are we going, then?"

"We'll head north. One of my men is out there. He flew out to inspect a crash site. I don't think that he had time to fly out before the storm closed in, and he wouldn't try it now. He knows his limitations. He'll be glad for some company if we can find him. It may be a week before this stuff clears enough to fly."

"Do you think we can find him?"

"Probably. I've got a good idea of where he landed. There aren't that many flat spots in this country. We've both got direction finding gear, so we shouldn't have any real problem."

They drove along quietly for a few minutes before Helga asked her next question. "Do you think they'll follow us?"

"It's unlikely, but not impossible," McKernan said. He wasn't trying to be reassuring. "Penderkarass may suspect that we aren't going back to the camp, and if he does, he'll try and come after us. He doesn't know where we're going, though. If we have enough of a lead on them, the wind may cover our tracks. It'll be pretty hard to follow us then. That's why I've kept off the radio. There isn't anybody close enough to help us out, and they might be able to get a direction fix on us."

"How much of a lead do we need?"

"Too much, I'm afraid. This isn't Earth. The buggy leaves a pretty deep track in the sand. Most of the stuff in the air is pretty fine. There isn't enough air pressure to lift anything heavier. It'll take a long time for our tracks to fill in. That's why I hope they went back to camp to wait for us."

Helga saw the grim look on McKernan's face and realized that if anything he was being optimistic in his appraisal of the situation. The earlier mood of relief had evaporated. Instead, she left him to the difficult business of driving. The storm was getting worse and the light was beginning to fail, though it was still only three in the afternoon. Against his better judgment, McKernan was forced to turn on the headlight to spot their path. Not doing so would have forced them to a crawl of a few kilometers an hour.

"Gaeretts should be about a hundred kilometers north of here. That's about eight hours driving if the storm

doesn't get any worse. Do you think that you can spell me
for a while on the driving. I don't want to stop if we can
avoid it."

"Yes, I think so. It doesn't look too hard."

"It's just like driving a car. Maybe simpler. There's a two
speed automatic transmission. This little lever on the dash
makes it go forwards or back. The pedals are just like on a
car except that there are two throttles set close together.
That's so you can drive just one side's wheels if you get
stuck.   Normally you push them down with one foot
because they're set so close together.   There's only one
brake pedal. Think you've got it."

"Yes. I can do it."

"Good. Watch me for a bit, now. We've got to go down
into one of those dried up valleys, shortly. I'll get us down
there because that will be kind of tricky, but after we're
down, you can drive. It should be pretty easy going then.
We just follow the valley floor for about sixty kilometers."

The valley came up on them quickly. Only at the last
minute did McKernan see the lip and brake them to a halt in
the loose sand at the top. They continued to skid forward in
the treacherous stuff until they finally stopped only a few
meters from the edge.

He paused and looked at the map for a moment, trying
to pick a place for their descent. the ground they were on
sloped towards the valley, before dropping off steeply to
the floor fifty meters below. McKernan made up his mind
and started to back the buggy up, but the wheels slipped in
the fine sand, spinning wildly. The rear of the buggy broke
loose, taking them closer to the edge as they slipped
sideways.

They hung helpless for a moment, and then they began
to move forwards as he used both feet to alternately feed
power to the wheels on either side. Cautiously he drove

them along the rim of the valley until he found firm ground where they could move back a few dozen meters from the edge.

They followed the lip for about a kilometer until McKernan found what he was looking for, a low spot on the rim where the wall had broken loose to form a slide that led onto the valley floor. It was steep going, and the slope was treacherous, unconsolidated material, but the map didn't show another spot for kilometers.

"Hold on. This is going to be rough."

He drove onto the slope, but from there on he wasn't driving, only trying to keep them from turning sideways and rolling over. They could hear rocks and debris bouncing against the outside of the buggy as their descent started a landslide, but in a moment it was over, and they were on the valley floor.

McKernan stopped the buggy and caught his breath. His knuckles were white where they had clutched the steering wheel. "That was hairier than I thought it would be. Do you feel like driving now?"

"After that last bit, I'm not so sure," Helga answered, but she was already getting up to trade places.

They changed seats and McKernan said, "Okay. Take it slow." Helga started the buggy moving tentatively, but after a few minutes she relaxed and drove with more confidence. "I'm going to try and get some sleep now, but if you have any trouble, wake me up."

The valley floor was relatively flat and crater free, and Helga was soon making good time, almost twenty kilometers an hour. Curiously, the dust wasn't as thick in the valley as it had been above on the rim. The steep sides were giving some protection from the wind keeping the air close to the floor relatively clear. It was a small blessing, but a welcome one. It was pitch dark in the valley, and without headlights, they would have been forced to stop. As it was, their universe extended only the width of the narrow valley and a few meters before and behind them. Above, the dust blew in a layer only a few meters overhead.

Despite having only a few hours of sleep in the last thirty six, McKernan had difficulty resting. Though flat, the valley floor was anything but smooth, and they bounced around quite a bit in the low Martian gravity. Mostly he napped for a few minutes at a time, checking on Helga in his waking moments.

They had gone forty some kilometers down the valley when Helga alerted him, "Erik, look behind us."

"I know," he said, emotion drained from his voice. For the last few minutes he had been looking into the big mirror that hung just outside the window on his side. At first he hadn't been certain. It could have been an illusion brought on by fatigue and the poor visibility. It wasn't an illusion, though. He was convinced of that. What he was were the faint beams of four powerful headlights following them.

"It's Penderkarass. We've only got about a kilometer's lead."

17

"Keep going," McKernan said as he watched the baleful eyes of the headlights follow them. "As long as they keep moving, we're okay. There's no way for Penderkarass to fire at us from inside the buggy, and I don't think that they're about to stop to get out. There's too much of a chance of our slipping away if they do."

Helga only nodded, but her concentration centered on her driving. She stared through the windshield with a look of determination on her face. They were bumping along the valley floor at a good clip, almost thirty kilometers an hour. At every bump the buggy threatened to get airborne. rising and falling with the slow motion undulations characteristic of the Martian gravity.

McKernan pulled out the topographical map and studied it intently. Trapped within the confines of the valley there was no place for them to run. If they were going to get away they would have to get back up to the surface where they stood a chance of getting lost in the poor visibility.

One thing was certain, his little automatic wasn't any sort of a match for the arsenal that Penderkarass was carrying. He had specifically chosen the weapon for its lack of penetrating power. The inside of a pressurized building was no place to be carrying a weapon that could blow a hole through someone and keep on going. The rationale had been right at the time, but at the moment he would have preferred the carbine or even the cannon of a revolver that he had carried earlier.

The choice wasn't there, so he concentrated on finding a way up and out of the valley. By his reckoning they were roughly twenty five kilometers from where Gaeretts waited with the plane.   If they could reach him, they would probably be safe. If not, they were in trouble.

"The map shows a narrow crack leading out of the valley. I've no idea of how steep it is, but it shouldn't be too far ahead. When I give the word, turn hard to the right and head straight up the crack. It's probably our only chance of getting away. They've gained a little on us. It's only a matter of time if we don't get out of here."

"Okay," Helga said calmly. She hadn't even suggested that they trade places, realizing that the time it would take would allow their pursuers to catch up with them.

"It'll probably be pretty rough, but don't worry about that. Just punch it, and once we start up, don't stop for anything."

McKernan kept his eye on the left wall of the valley which was just barely illuminated by their headlamps. The crack the map showed wasn't very wide. In the dark they could easily miss it, yet they didn't dare to slow down.

"There it is," he cried out as he pointed. "Okay, turn."

Helga cranked the wheel, and the buggy turned towards the valley wall, leaning, almost threatening to tip over. The wheels spun as the vehicle slid sideways. Then they caught and the buggy headed for the blackness that marked the crack.

As the headlights flashed up the depression, they picked up a boulder strewn talus sloping up steeply towards the valley rim. The angle would have been impossible on earth. Only the lesser gravity of Mars kept the loose material of the slope from giving way in the landslide.

The buggy hit the slope with a crunch, the nose of the vehicle bouncing up in the air. As the rear wheels hit the talus, they began to slip and spin throwing sand and rocks backwards, but the buggy kept moving from its momentum.

Helga was driving well, using both feet to work the throttles, trying desperately to keep the wheels biting on the slope instead of spinning uselessly.

The first thirty meters went well, but then they started to slow as the slope steepened and the wheels slipped more and more. At any moment it seemed like they would stop and begin to slide back down into the arms of Penderkarass and Orloff, but they kept moving forward, maintaining at least some momentum.

The wheels were now sending a shower of rocks down the slope. In the mirror McKernan couldn't see anything but dust and sand from the slide that they had started. Suddenly he felt the whole slope start to give way beneath them.

"Punch it. Give it all she's got," he shouted as he looked behind.

The tires spun furiously, and then the buggy lurched forward as the wheels caught. In the glare of the headlights he could see the rim of the valley only a few meters ahead of them. Suddenly the tires gripped solid ground and the buggy sped forward up over the rim.

For a long moment they were airborne, floating almost gently in the Martian gravity. Then they came down with a sickening thump. Below and behind them McKernan could hear the snap and scrape of metal giving way. They kept on rolling, but the buggy now tilted precariously towards the left rear wheel.

"I think we've broken the suspension," McKernan said. "Keep on going. I don't think that this is any place to stop."

Helga kept driving, but it was obvious from her expression that the buggy was no longer handling properly. Their speed had slowed to ten kilometers an hour, and with every bump a protest of scraping metal came from the rear.

"I don't think that I can keep this thing moving much longer. It keeps wanting to turn to the left. Is there anything that we can do?" Helga asked.

"I'll have to get out and look. I don't think that Penderkarass can get up the way we did. We made too much of a mess of it. Most of the slope gave way beneath us. I don't think that there's another way up for a buggy for five kilometers or so in either direction. We've got some lead on them, at least. Pull up behind that crater and I'll see how bad it is."

Helga did as he directed. As McKernan zipped up the front of his surface suit, she said, "I guess that I made a mess of driving. I'm sorry I broke the buggy."

McKernan grinned. "You did fine. As well as I could have, considering. If you hadn't tromped on it at the end, we would have gotten caught in the slide." Helga brightened a little. "You handled yourself well. Don't worry about it."

"Erik. What happens if you can't fix the buggy? What happens to us then?" she asked.

"If it's busted so badly that we can't move, we get some rest and wait until morning, then we take ourselves a nice, long hike. Gaeretts is only fifteen or twenty kilometers that way," he said, pointing with his head. "With luck we could get there before nightfall. But we don't even know if we have to walk yet, so don't worry."

McKernan put on his helmet and buttoned up his suit. He used the little flexible airlock on the side of the buggy to get out so that Helga wouldn't lose pressure inside. The wind seemed to have died out a little, and some of the bigger particles of dust had started to settle out. He rapped on the window and signaled Helga to turn out the headlights. The visibility wasn't that much better, but he saw no point in advertising their position.

Before he turned to examining the damage, he scanned the horizon behind them. There wasn't any sign of Penderkarass or Orloff. McKernan suspected that he was right about the defile being blocked after them.

With some satisfaction he turned to the buggy. There things didn't look so good. In the light of his helmet lamp he could pick out the damage. They must have come down hard on a rock when they had landed. The big, bulbous, balloon tire had flattened and the shock absorber had collapsed under the force of the impact. Martian gravity might be weaker, but the masses involved were still the same. On earth the van would have weighed close to four metric tons. They had come down awfully hard.

Mars buggies were rugged vehicles. Neither a flat tire nor the collapsed shock would have put them out of action. Unfortunately, the damage extended further. The strut holding the wheel on was cracked badly and bent upwards. McKernan didn't think that it would last long if they tried to drive on it.

Discouraged, McKernan climbed back into the buggy. In answer to Helga's questioning glance he said, "The buggy has pretty much had it. I don't think that it'll go more than a couple of kilometers. We'll have to walk the rest of the way."

"Do we stand much of a chance?" Helga asked. Her voice was flat and emotionless.

"Don't take it so seriously. Be thankful that you've got a good suit. If you had one of those rental suits we'd be in trouble, but Goldschmidt knows what he's doing. I've known people who have spent weeks in a suit. It can be pretty uncomfortable, but it's not really dangerous. With luck, we'll only be out about sixteen hours. Prospectors do that all the time. The buggy has a couple of spare air tanks and an emergency tent, so we're in good shape. The storm seems to be dying out, as well. I think that if we wait until daybreak that the visibility should be improved. The best think we can do is get some rest now."

"Erik?" Helga asked. "Are you sorry that I got you into this?"

"You didn't actually get me into this. It's my job," McKernan said with a laugh. "If anything, you've made it easier, though I haven't handled things as well as I could have. I know who killed Morrison, and what's better, I've got proof. Penderkarass isn't going to get away, nor is Orloff. My only regret is that you've been put in danger."

It wasn't easy in the seats of the buggy, but they managed to snuggle together in some semblance of comfort, with Helga resting her head on his shoulder.

McKernan's suit timer went off a little before dawn waking them. They were both stiff from the cramped quarters of the buggy, but otherwise cheerful.

"Feel up to a long walk?" McKernan asked as they ate a meal of concentrates.

"Not really," Helga replied. "Not if all I get to eat is this stuff."

"I'll buy you a big dinner when we get back to the city."

"Well, with all the exercise I won't have to worry about my figure."

"I never have," McKernan said. "I think that we'd better get going if we're going to find Gaeretts by nightfall. If I baby this thing along, we may be able to ride at least a few kilometers before we have to get out and walk."

He started up the buggy's turbine, letting it warm up for a few minutes. While they waited, Helga went back to the small lavatory tucked into one wall of the buggy. There was a sharp crack followed by a hiss. In the front of the buggy an alarm sounded. "What's happening?" Helga cried.

"Get your helmet on. Don't waste time. We've been holed," McKernan shouted back. He was already scrambling out of the driver's seat towards his own helmet.

With it secured, he reached out for Helga and pulled her to the floor, checking to make sure that her helmet was properly sealed. To her questioning glance he pointed up at the wall of the buggy. A hole had appeared in the side about the size of a poker chip.

McKernan placed his helmet in contact with Helga's and said, "We're being shot at. Penderkarasss must have gotten out of the valley somehow. He's taking pot shots at us with a rifle." They both felt another impact that proved that.

"I think he got the turbine with that one. We've got to get out of here. The sides of the buggy can't stop the bullets. There's an emergency exit on the side away from him. I'm going to open it. When I do, get out fast. Keep close to the ground. Crawl. Try to find something to hide behind and wait for me."

"What are you going to do? she asked with concern.

"I'm going after him."

"All you've got is that little pistol. You don't stand a chance, Erik."

"It's the only one we've got. If I don't get him, he'll get us. He can pick us off from a couple of kilometers away with that gun of his. Now get ready. I'm going to pop the hatch."

McKernan hit the release lever on the emergency exit. What little air that remained in the cabin of the buggy rushed out in a cloud of condensation. He practically shoved Helga out before following her, rolling as he hit the ground. He came up on his belly with the little automatic in his hand.

Using one of the balloon tires of the buggy for cover he watched as Helga crawled off across the sand. There was a crater close by, a meter deep and two across. With relief he saw her flop over the rim into the relative safety of the interior.

The ground dipped slightly to the left, so McKernan worked his way down the slope moving away from where he thought the shots had come from. He found his own bit of shelter and crouched behind it to catch his breath. While he waited, he scanned the horizon trying to pinpoint Penderkarass.

He saw a flash low towards the west about three hundred meters off from his position. A moment later he saw the left front tire of the buggy go flat. They still must believe that Helga and he were in the buggy, McKernan thought. That was good.

He waited for another flash, but it was a long time in coming. When it did, it was followed by an explosion that shattered the buggy, scattering debris for a kilometer. Entranced, he watched pieces of metal and plastic fall in a slow motion rain. The tanks of liquid oxygen and liquid methane that had powered the turbine must have been punctured at the same time. They had been lucky that Penderkarass hadn't shot them the first time.

For a long time things were quiet as the pieces of the buggy came down. There wasn't any sound, but he could see the splashes of dust where the bigger chunks fell.

The wind had died down while they had slept, and the air close to the ground was fairly clear as the bigger particles of dust had settled out. For the first time since they had gotten up, McKernan took a good look around. Overhead he could still see a layer of haze about a hundred meters up, lit from the underside by the ruddy rays of the rising sun. The whole sky seemed to glow with a pinkish light. Another time he might have been caught in wonder, but the lawman had more important things on his mind.

Two figures in surface suits had risen from the area where the shots had come. From the way one of them cradled his right arm he could tell that it was Penderkarass. In his left hand he carried a long barreled weapon, a rifle with a scope. As far as McKernan could tell, Orloff was unarmed, though he was probably still carrying the revolver.

They moved carefully towards what remained of the buggy. They might believe that McKernan and Helga were dead, but Penderkarass's jungle bred caution was still with him. McKernan wondered what the range of his own weapon was. Certainly he couldn't count on accuracy at anything more than ten meters. He'd have to get closer than that if he was to have any chance.

Penderkarass's attention seemed centered on the buggy. McKernan took advantage of that to work his way around them so that he would be flanking them as they neared the vehicle. He wasn't careful enough, though any motion at all would have stood out against the dead plains of Mars.

He saw Penderkarass ponderously bring up the rifle using his right forearm as a rest for the barrel. The lawman dove for cover expecting as any moment to feel the slug rip through his body in the brief instant before unconsciousness and death took him.

The bullet didn't come. Penderkarass seemed to be waiting for his shot, picking it with care. McKernan was completely exposed, but still the rifle wavered uncertainly. Able to stand the suspense no longer, McKernan squeezed off a shot from his gun. It was a bad shot uphill at a range of almost fifty meters. He saw a spurt of dust twenty meters behind the two men and at least a dozen off to one side.

The shot settled Penderkarass's mind. McKernan saw the flash and waited for the impact. It never came. He waited for a second shot, but when he looked up he saw Penderkarass fumbling with the rifle.

McKernan realized in amazement that it was a single shot weapon. The implication took only a moment to sink in. He scrambled out of the dust and began to run towards Penderkarass. The outlaw saw him but continued to work at loading his rifle, hampered by having only one useable hand.

Thirty meters, then twenty separated them. Penderkarass had the rifle loaded and was raising it towards his shoulder again. McKernan stopped, raised his own weapon. The barrel of the rifle swung up. He could see the hole in the end of the barrel looking like a cavern. It was pointing at his feet, then his knees. His own gun swung up to Penderkarass's waist, then to his chest.

McKernan squeezed the trigger, emptying the clip. He saw the holes sprout in the front of Penderkarass's suit, but the rifle continued on its upward course. He could see the look of hatred on Penderkarass's face through the faceplate of his helmet. Then the face went slack.

Penderkarass slumped backwards. There was a flash as the rifle discharged itself as he fell, then the two of them, man and weapon, lay sprawled in the red dust of Mars.

McKernan had forgotten about Orloff in confronting his first adversary. Now he turned towards the geologist. The man hadn't stood his ground. Already he was running off in the direction of the valley. McKernan raised his pistol, then realized that it was empty. He grabbed the rifle from the ground next to Penderkarass.

It was a strange, unfamiliar weapon to McKernan. It bore more relation to a target weapon than to a hunting rifle. The long barrel seemed to stretch out forever, but the balance was perfect. He fumbled with the bolt action of the breech trying to insert a round. There was a scope on the rifle, specially modified to be used through the faceplate of a helmet, but Penderkarass had hung it from the right side so that he could fire the gun with his uninjured left hand.

Orloff was a tiny figure when McKernan finally got the rifle loaded and raised. The scope was useless, so he used the sites along the top of the barrel to aim on the fleeing geologist. Even without the scope it was an easy shot with Orloff silhouetted against the pink of the sky. He couldn't miss.

McKernan let the rifle drop. There had been enough killing already, he thought. His own anger had been concentrated against Penderkarass, the man who had actually pulled the trigger against Morrison. That had been resolved. He would leave Orloff to be picked up by Konstantin. He turned and walked towards where Helga was waiting.

18

"Erik, are you all right?" Helga asked as she ran to him.

"Yes, I'm okay. Penderkarass is dead."

"I saw," she said without comment. Her eyes were hard as if she had seen a side of him that she wished had remained hidden. "What do we do now?"

"We start walking. How much air do you have in your suit tanks?" McKernan asked.

"The gauge says eighteen hours."

"Mine says twenty," McKernan said. He was bigger than the woman, but not by that much. Their rates of oxygen consumption wouldn't differ by much. The amount of time on the gauges was only an estimate. How quickly they actually used up their supply would depend on how much they exerted themselves. The ground between them and Gaeretts wasn't the easiest.

"Do we have enough?"

"Maybe. It'll be close. I had counted on taking along some extra tanks from the buggy and a survival tent in case we didn't find Gaeretts by nightfall. It's too late for that now. We'll have to make it by dark or not make it at all."

"What about Orloff and the other buggy?" Helga asked hopefully.

"He's got too much of a lead on us by now. He'll be gone before we could get to the buggy." They stood silently for a moment, then McKernan reached out to her and said, "We'd better get going."

They started walking across the plain heading north. "Take it easy," McKernan warned her. "We've got a long walk ahead of us. Conserve your energy and breath. Most importantly, don't let yourself get winded. If you feel yourself short of breath, signal me and we'll rest. And don't talk unless it's necessary."

"Is it really that close?" Helga asked.

McKernan only nodded. Out of habit he let himself fall into a slow, steady gait that ate up kilometers with a minimum of energy. Helga, less accustomed to the gravity, found the rhythm harder to adapt to. McKernan could see that she was consuming oxygen faster than he was, but there wasn't anything that he could do about it. All he could do was hope that eventually she would fall into a smoother pace.

The first few kilometers were fairly easy, and they made good time. The ground was level, and the sand only a few centimeters deep. Only a few craters obstructed their path and, these they could go around without losing much time. Only a small portion of the sunlight filtered through the layers of dust that hung over their heads like a ceiling, giving the landscape a strange cast like some reddish vision of the plains of hell. McKernan found it oppressive. It was hard to be optimistic in such a gloomy scene.

McKernan had managed to save the topological map of the area. By chance he had stuck it in one of the pockets of his surface suit the night before. Without it they would have been in bad shape. As it was, finding their position from landmarks was fairly easy as long as they had light enough to see by.

The one bad thing the map showed was a patch of broken ground between them and Gaeretts. It didn't look like much on the map, but they would have to climb a couple of hundred meters through rough country. It would take a lot of time, and a lot of their oxygen to get through to the other side.

When they got to the end of the plain and the start of the hills they took a rest. McKernan figured that they weren't doing badly. They still had four more hours of air than they had hour of light left. Helga had finally caught the right stride after the first couple of hours.

Sitting on a rock looking at what faced them the next couple of hours, they paused. McKernan took a suck of water from the tank in his helmet. Helga hadn't refilled hers. He didn't envy her. He could tell by the way that she licked her lips, that her mouth already tasted like cotton.

"How much farther?" Helga asked when he pulled out the map to study it.

"About six kilometers if he landed where I think he did. It won't be as easy as the last six, though. Mostly up and down. If there was a way around it, I'd take it, but we'd have to go too far out of our way. I haven't been through here before. I don't really know what to expect."

Helga didn't say anything. There wasn't much to say. Either they'd make it or they wouldn't. McKernan had been worried about her. She had been through a lot in the last few days. She had held up well. He knew that she had seen some rough things in Burma; he had been there himself. But it was one thing to see things happen around you, quite another when they were happening to you. She was pretty tough inside, as tough as himself. He just hoped that she would be tough enough.

He realized that she had been watching him. There was more than curiosity in her face, more like a need to get inside his head. When she saw that he was looking at her in turn, she grinned.

"You could have shot Orloff this morning, couldn't you?" she asked when the moment had passed.

"Yes. I had a bullet in the rifle, and I had him in my sights. I don't think that I would have missed."

"Why didn't you shoot?"

"I'm not sure. I should have. We might have found the other buggy. He'll get his, sooner or later, though. I've got enough evidence on him. He'll never hold a decent job again. I'm not sure what will be done with him and the rest of the people involved when they get back to Earth, but they're all pretty much washed up professionally. They'll never work off Earth again."

"Is that enough?" Helga asked.

"Who knows. I'm not sure that I'm qualified to judge."

"You made a judgment about Penderkarass. You wanted to kill him."

"You're right. I wanted to kill Penderkarass. It doesn't make any difference that in the end it was him or me. I wanted to kill him. To Orloff, killing Morrison was just an abstraction, a detail in his plan. That doesn't make him any less guilty of course, but it is a difference. Penderkarass was the one that pulled the trigger. He watched Morrison over the sight of his rifle, and then he shot him, coldly and calmly. He knew what he was doing, he knew what it meant to take a human life. He'd done it enough times before. He was like all of us that were in Burma and all the other wars before or since. He'd lost his innocence. He knew what he was doing and he liked it, no guilt, no remorse, not even a little regret that it was necessary. If I hadn't killed him, he would have killed again sooner or later. Probably sooner."

"I was in Burma, too," Helga said. "War didn't do that to me or a lot of others."

"Yeah, but you didn't kill. I did."

The climb through the hills was a long and arduous one. The hills themselves presented a maze of passages and passes through which they had to pick their way. Though they had started up before noon, it was after five when they finally won free of the rough ground, and the dim light indicated that the sun would soon be setting.

McKernan had hoped that once they were on the north side of the hills that they would be able to see the plane where Gaeretts had holed up during the storm, but as they made their last descent, those hopes were dashed. If Gaeretts was in fact still out there, he had landed farther north than McKernan had figured, and the plane was hidden beyond the horizon.

"Can't you get him on the radio?" Helga asked.

"I'm afraid that it doesn't work that way. All communications is line of site on Mars. There's no ionosphere to scatter radio back around the horizon. And our suit radios don't have enough power to raise the relay satellites in orbit. We'll just have to keep walking until we're in range."

"What if he's not there?" Helga asked. McKernan read the note of fatigue in her voice. He wondered how long she would be able to go on. She was beginning to lose the will to continue.

"If he's not there, we're dead. But he's out there, all right. The storm hasn't cleared enough for him to take off. Gaeretts is an old Mars hand. He's learned to be careful. He wouldn't mind sitting still for a few days to wait the storm out. He's done it plenty of times before. We'll just have to keep going until we can find some high ground closer to him and try to raise him on the radio."

"Let's get going while we still have the light." McKernan rose and put out his hand to help Helga. She followed him up with some reluctance, then almost collapsed when he let go.

"How much air do you have left?" McKernan asked sternly.

Helga hesitated as if uncertain what he meant. Finally she replied. "The gauge has been in the yellow for the last fifteen minutes."

"You should have told me," McKernan said angrily.

Mechanically he looked at his own gauge. It still showed him with three hours of air left. Familiarity and experience had allowed him to use less of the precious oxygen. He cursed himself for not keeping a closer watch on her air supply.

"Sit down again. I'm going to transfer some of the oxygen from my tank to yours. That should give us each about another hour and a half before we run out."

"Don't, Erik," Helga said as she pushed away his hands as he tried to connect a piece of tubing to the regulator on her backpack. "I can't go on any longer. Save the air for yourself. That way you might have a chance."

McKernan protested, "Don't be a fool. If Gaeretts is still out there at all, he's less than five kilometers away. The ground is level, we can both make it that far easily with the air that we've got left. I'm not going to leave you here, and if I have to carry you we might not make it."

He tried again to make the connection and this time Helga didn't try to interfere. Whether his reasoning had convinced her, or whether she had just given up caring, he didn't know. He was beginning to have doubts himself whether Gaeretts was out there, but he hadn't come so far just to stop short.

He transferred half of his remaining supply to Helga's tanks. The fresh supply of oxygen revived her, and she smiled wanly at him as he disconnected the hose. He helped her up, and they started walking north again.

The terrain was easier, but it grew progressively darker as the sun set. Before they had gone a kilometer they were forced to turn on their helmet lights to pick their way. McKernan was worried. With the fall of darkness, their chances of finding the plane were decreasing drastically. They couldn't even tell exactly where they were without being able to spot landmarks. All they could do was keep heading in the direction that McKernan's gyrocompass indicated as north, and keep trying to raise Gaeretts on the radio.

Three more kilometers, and they still hadn't raised him. McKernan's gauge gave him half an hour before it touched the yellow. Fifteen minutes after that it would reach the red, but he wouldn't be around long to worry about that. He let Helga rest for a moment and climbed a small knoll about five meters above the plain. Keying his transmitter to the distress frequency, he sent a message.

Moments later the reply came back startlingly loud and clear. "McKernan? Is that you?" Gaeretts seemed out of breath and excited. "I've been expecting you. Konstantin said that you were probably heading my way. He's got Orloff at Camp #3."

"There's time for that later. We're low on air. Where are you?"

"I'm in a little depression at grid reference K 7. That's probably why you can't see me. I've got all my lights on. The direction finder says that you're to the southwest. You can't be far. Your signal is coming in loud and clear."

McKernan stared into the darkness towards the northeast trying to pick out the plane's lights. "It's no good. I can't see you. Either the dust is obscuring you or there's a hill in the way."

"Okay. I'll fire a flare. Tell me if you spot it."

McKernan kept his eyes open, but saw nothing. "I didn't see it. It must have gone off up in the damned dust. We've only got about half an hour left. I'll head towards you. You can keep giving us a radio fix every couple of minutes in case we go wrong."

"Okay. I'll be waiting."

McKernan hurried down the hill towards Helga. "Let's get going. I've found him. He's over that way, probably not more than a couple of kilometers."

McKernan tried to raise Gaeretts again, but failed. He had needed that little bit of elevation provided by the knoll to get within line of sight. If what Gaeretts had said about being in a depression was true, there was some piece of intervening high ground that was in the way. It was probably only a few meters high, but that was enough to cause them problems."

Helga had wanted to race ahead, but McKernan kept them to a slower pace. It wasn't the time to run out of oxygen, not when they were so close to rescue. As they walked he kept an eye on the gauge in his helmet, watching the needle creep closer to the yellow.

His own needle was only its own width away from that line when he felt that they had started up a rise. It was shallow, hardly noticeable, but they were going up, all the same. Any moment, McKernan thought, they'd reach the top and there would be the plane lit up like a Christmas tree.

Helga tripped and stumbled on lose rock. McKernan bent down to help her and when he straightened he saw a tiny light bobbing towards them. A moment later he could make out the form of Gaeretts in his surface suit moving towards them.

"When you dropped out of communications I got worried. Thought that you might be lower on air that you said, so I got a couple of tanks and headed out to meet you. The plane is just down the hill about five hundred meters. Can you make it?"

"You better charge up both our tanks first. I'm running right on the yellow," McKernan said as he sunk next to Helga.

19

It was two days before the storm had cleared enough for McKernan to fly the plane back to the city. During that time they caught up on their sleep and took turns playing gin with Gaeretts. They also managed to finish off the flask of vodka Gaeretts had brought with him in disregard of the regulations governing flying on Mars.

With a little rest, Helga had sprung back, and was lamenting the fact that she hadn't had her camera with her to cover one of the best stories of her career. McKernan's protests that it had almost been her last story went unheeded.

The lawman didn't spend all his time in idleness. By radio, he was in contact with his constables and with McAndrews. Konstantin had arrived at Camp #3 about twenty hours after they had left. He had taken a statement from the night attendant and done some investigating on his own. He'd managed to turn up quite a bit of evidence and was ready and waiting when Orloff returned to the camp. The geologist had lost his nerve and surrendered without a struggle. Later, Konstantin had gone out with a buggy and recovered the bodies of Guineri and Penderkarass's henchmen as well as their weapons.

He had also uncovered the names of a number of the other conspirators, including the man who had cracked the safe in the claims office. Except for three men who had already returned to Earth, all had been arrested, either at Mars City by Ferris and Kaminski, or by men McKernan had deputized from Anglo Martian or other corporations.

From what McAndrews had told him, the Trust Authority and the Trust Council were in an uproar, and the whole matter was being referred back to the UN General Assembly. McKernan didn't particularly care. He had done his job, and the results had turned out better than he had hoped. Most of the big fish had been caught, which was more than he had ever expected. His only regret was that the superintendent of Camp #3 had gotten himself killed. Guineri had turned out to be completely ignorant of what Orloff and Penderkarass had been up to.

A hearing was held three days after they had returned, and it was a long and trying affair made worse by the fact that the Trust Council on Earth had been linked in by radio with a half an hour delay in response due to the speed of light. McKernan was only too glad to get it over with and head for Finnegan's to meet Helga.

"How did it go?" she asked, when he and McAndrews joined her in the booth.

McKernan signaled for two drinks, and he wasn't at all surprised when Finnegan brought them over and slid into the booth next to McAndrews. The hearing had been the biggest thing to happen on Mars since the first landing. All of the permanent residents had been following the events closely since the story had broken. It was clear that there were going to be some changes in how the planet was run, and they wanted to find out all about it.

"It went about as well as can be expected. United Semi has lost their license for mining on Mars and all their claims have been appropriated. Any of their men who can't find work are being sent back to Earth. That's a raw deal for some of them, because most of them were completely ignorant of what was going on, but the Trust Council is making a big show of things to prove that they haven't been corrupted. As it is, half a dozen of the council members are quitting for health reasons."

"Is that all that's going to happen to United Semi? That's really only a slap on the wrist," Helga complained.

"We weren't able to prove that any of the top management on Earth were involved, or even had any idea of what was going on. I doubt if we ever will. But along with losing their license on Mars, they have also been placed under a five year ban on filing new claims anywhere the UN has jurisdiction. That means the seabed, the moon, even the asteroids if they start mining out there. They aren't ruined, but Orloff's little venture has cost them billions of dollars, at least. I don't think that the stock holders are going to be very pleased about what has happened.

"As for Orloff, he's being sent back to earth for the murder of Morrison. The Trust Council has had quite a time deciding who, if anybody, has jurisdiction in the case. It was finally decided that because Morrison was an Australian national, that they have the right to prosecute. Legally, that's pretty shaky, but the Aussie's are small enough that it was politically acceptable. None of the big powers wanted to get involved in this mess, and there wasn't any objection from any of the third or fourth world countries. Orloff has run out of friends, and no one wanted to see him go free."

"What's going to happen next time?" Finnegan asked quietly. He sipped his whiskey as he eyed first McKernan and then McAndrews.

"We hope that there won't be a next time," McAndrews said. "But obviously Mars can't continue to be run in such a loose manner. As the representative of the corporations, I've recommended that some form of limited self rule be adopted for Mars with an elected assembly chosen by the long term residents of the planet. The assembly would be allowed to make laws with regards to criminal acts, though they would have no jurisdiction over the granting of claims or licenses. Personally, that was all I thought that I could get away with. The UN gets a large share of its revenue from Martian mining, and they're not about to give that up."

"Actually, I don't know how well my idea was received by the Trust Council. I'm afraid that they found it, well, revolutionary. But it seems to me that the corporations might well get a more reasonable deal from the people that live up here, than from some bureaucrats who have never set foot off earth."

"What was Anglo Martian's response to your proposal?" McKernan asked wryly.

"Well, you can't accuse me of ignoring the lessons of our last three centuries of colonial debacles. The permanent population of Mars is growing every year. We can't expect to keep ruling it from Earth forever. Frankly, I'm not sure that I'll ever go back to earth. The low gravity is good for my heart. I'd have a rough time if I ever went back to Earth, or so my doctor says. So you can see that I'm not entirely without some self interest in this matter."

"Don't let Otis fool you," McKernan said. "I think that he has plans of becoming the first prime minister of Mars or whatever we decide to call it. He's already been appointed governor."

"Now really, Erik. That appointment is just temporary until the Trust Council can find someone to replace Powell."

"Did Powell get the ax?" Helga asked.

"Not exactly," McKernan explained. "He's resigned for health reasons. There seems to have been a lot of poor health going around the Trust Authority lately. Powell played it pretty cleverly. There wasn't any evidence against him. But all his support is gone from the Council. He'll go back to Earth and retire on his pension, but at least he'll be gone. And for the time being, Otis is in charge. I think that it may be some time before the Authority gets itself straightened out, so the position may well become more or less permanent."

"I guess that congratulations are in order then," Finnegan said. Scurrying back to the bar he fetched a dust covered bottle from deep behind the bar. The label was in Gaelic, but "aged 18 years" was written on a label around the neck and the tax stamp was twenty years old. Finnegan poured a shot for each of them, and they stood and toasted McAndrews. He saluted them in turn and said, "To Mars."

It was some time later that McAndrews left and Finnegan retired behind the bar. McKernan could feel a tenseness in Helga, and he wasn't surprised when she said, "Erik, I've got to go back to earth."

"When?"

"Tonight. There's a ship leaving at eight."

"Rather sudden, isn't it?" McKernan said, not concealing a trace of bitterness.

"I didn't know myself until a few hours ago. There's some sort of brushfire war or revolution going on in Africa. My editor wants me to cover it. I'm sorry, Erik. I would liked to have stayed a little longer at least, but my story is done and it's time for me to get back to earth. We both knew that it would come to this sooner or later."

McKernan silently drained his glass. After a pause, he said, "Yes, I suppose we both did. I guess I just didn't want to face up to it. I had hoped that you might consider staying."

"I thought about it, but Mars is your planet, not mine," Helga said

"It could be. There's a place for you here."

"I don't think so. Not now. Not yet. I'm good at what I do, and I like doing it. I like to think that I do it better than most. I can't turn my back on that, Erik. There's nothing more for me to do here, not what I'm good at. There is down on Earth. I've got to go. It's part of me, and I can't ignore it. I can't stay here anymore than you can give up your job and return to earth with me. If you did, you'd end up hating me. Do you understand?"

McKernan smiled a tight lipped smile. "Yes, the hell of it is that I do understand. We've both put our jobs before everything, even ourselves. There's no changing that, I guess."

"Would you like me to see you off to the spaceport?" he asked at last.

"No. I still haven't packed yet. As I said, I didn't have much warning, and I wanted to tell you first. I owed you that much." She stood and McKernan had to get up to let her slide out of the booth. As she walked past him she turned and kissed him once. "If you and McAndrews ever pull off your revolution, maybe I'll be back someday. I'd like to do that."

"Take care. Don't get yourself caught in a crossfire." Her held his hand out towards her. She touched it and then turned to leave. He watched he as she disappeared through the doorway.

Later that night, McKernan returned to his hut feeling empty and alone. He hadn't even bothered to get drunk. There hadn't seemed much point in it. Without thinking, he went through the routine of checking the life support system and the oxygen plants. He reflected that he'd been neglecting them lately, though they didn't seem the worse for it.

He laid the automatic and the holster on the crate next to the bed and undressed hurriedly so that he could get under the blankets. One day soon he would have to see about insulating the place better. Turning off the lights he laid back and listened to the grains of sand abrading against the aluminum skin of the hut until he fell asleep.

THE END

SPECIAL PREVIEW!

THE LAWS OF MAGIC
By Greg Fowlkes
© 2010

Now available from The Fictional Press
www.TheFictionalPress.com

THE LAWS OF MAGIC

☆ ☆ ☆ ☆ ☆

WITHOUT LICENSE

As Egil Njalsson climbed the steps of the criminal courts building he wondered if it was really worth it. Eighteen months of practicing law on his own and here he was in his only suit, about to attend the preliminary hearing in a petty case for which with luck he would be able to recover his expenses. It wasn't even a paying client. The state would be picking up the tab for this one, and he'd ended up being the lawyer appointed by the court. At the moment it wasn't clear who would benefit most from the charity, the client or the lawyer. He hadn't had a case in three months and he'd just been eking out a living writing briefs for other lawyers. He could do that well enough. His technical background gave him a depth of knowledge most lawyers lacked when it came to cases involving points of science as well as law. If he hadn't had that he'd be starving.

He'd been thinking about that a lot lately; whether he had made the right decision giving up science and going into the law. At the time, with the aerospace industry in a depression in the early seventies, it had seemed like a good idea. Engineers were pumping gas and PhD's in physics were selling insurance. Being a lawyer had seemed like a good way to make money. A stable income, no ups and downs. He'd put in his time at law school and done well. After the grind at CalThaum, law school had been a snap. So here he was a lawyer barely making ends meet and his school mates, the ones who had stuck with science were all making it rich designing personal calculating engines and disk storage units.

He tried to put all these thoughts out of his mind as he passed through the big brass doors of the court house. After all, he did have a client to defend, and a duty to him. It wasn't easy, though. It wasn't, after all, a very important case. Just a charge of fortune telling and practicing the Art without a license. Minor offenses, probably not even any jail time involved. This wouldn't even be a trial today, just a plea and arranging of bail.

It wouldn't even have amounted to that if his client hadn't instisted on pleading not guilty. He'd met him at the county jail, an old man, one Jake Schmidts. He'd tried to talk him out of pleading not guilty, too. A guilty plea, a small fine, and they both could be done with it. His client, though, had turned out to be something of a character. So here he was.

It took an hour and a half before their case came up. The judge looked at him questioningly when he had pleaded not guilty, but thankfully had released his client on his own recognizance when he indicated he had a permanent address. It was over in five minutes.

They got the release papers and the court date from the bailiff. Egil started to head out when he noticed that his client seemed lost and disoriented by it all. "Do you have car fare home?"

"No," Schmidts said. "I didn't have any money on me when they came and arrested me. Not a cent."

"Which way do you live?"

The old man gave an address on Fair Oaks Street. It wasn't far out of his way. Neither one of them lived in the best part of town.

"I can give you a lift," Egil said.

"That's kind of you, Mr. Njalsson," Schmidts said. The mister was ironic. The arrest report hadn't given an age, just "somewhere around seventy." As far as Egil could tell that might have been off by a decade or two.

The address turned out to be a sort of second hand junk store. The operative word was junk. If the pieces in the dirty window were the best of the lot then Egil could see how Schmidts qualified as indigent.

"Thanks for the ride. I've a beer inside if you'd like."

Njalsson looked at his watch. It wasn't too early to start drinking, at least just a beer. The work at the office would wait. He had to talk to Schmidts anyway to prepare a case. Besides, the old man seemed to want to pay him back for the ride.

If anything, the shop was worse on the inside than it looked from the front. Odd bits of bric-a-brac were strewn around everywhere; most of it looking like it hadn't been moved or even dusted in twenty years. Broken down pieces of furniture were covered with moldering sheets.

The old man led him to the back and up some stairs to an apartment above the shop. The kitchen was cleaner, though still hardly spotless. Of course, Egil's own small apartment wasn't the neatest of place, either.

The refrigerator looked as old as Schmidt's, but the beer was cold. Schmidt's took out two and motioned him to a chair at the kitchen table.

"So what happens now, Mr. Njalsson?"

"The trial will be held on the date on the summons. The district attorney will call his witnesses and make his case. Then I'll make my case. The judge will then decide."

"No jury?" Schmidt's asked disappointedly.

"Not unless we've got a very strong case to present. This is a small matter. It's better left to a judge. A jury would be considered a waste of time, I'm afraid, and would probably result in a higher fine. Maybe even jail."

"So you think I'm guilty?"

"I don't think you have much of a case."

"That's different?"

"To a lawyer it is."

Schmidts snorted in disgust.

"I don't want to disillusion you, Mr. Schmidts, but you've got to face the facts. Do you have a license to practice Magic?"

"No."

"Did you tell the fortune of one Mrs. Einar Johnson?"

"Yes, and an ungrateful woman she is, too. Just because I told her the truth about that shifty salesman she thinks is going to marry her. He's just after her late husband's money."

Egil raised an eyebrow.

"It's the truth. I've been reading the cards longer than you've been alive, Mr. Njalsson, and I know what I'm doing. That salesman is the one that got her to swear out a complaint against me."

"It doesn't matter whether what you said was the truth or not. What matters is that you were practicing the Art without a license. Magic is a potentially dangerous business. It's not something that untrained people should be dealing with. That's what the law is about."

"What would you know about the Art, Mr. Lawyer?" Schmidts asked sharply.

"I know more than most, Mr. Schmidts. I studied applied metaphysics at the California Institute of Thaumaturgy for four years before going into the law. I've got a Bachelor's of Science degree. I've also got my practitioner's license from both the state of California and Wisconsin. I may not be the greatest practitioner of the Art, but I am competent enough to know what I am and am not capable of."

"So maybe you did study at a fancy school out west. Those scientists don't know everything. They think that they've discovered magic, but magic goes back. Way back. Back before Helmholtz and Gauss. Before the Egyptians and Babylonians. Magic is old, Mr. Njalsson, and the doctors and professors haven't learned half of it."

"And you have?" Egil asked sarcastically. He was getting annoyed at the old man's pretensions of knowledge. He was surprised, though, that Schmidts knew that the two physicists Helmholtz and Gauss had been instrumental in proving the scientific basis for magic.

"No. I'm no fool. I've been studying the Art all my life. I know what I know and I have a good idea of what I don't. What I do know is more than a youngster like you learns in four years at college, even if it is a fancy one."

"Look, Mr. Schmidts," Egil said. "This isn't working out. Maybe you should get yourself a different lawyer."

The old man looked at him in surprise, then shook his head. "No. I guess you were just telling me the way it is. I may not like it, but I can't fault you for telling the truth."

"Okay. Is there anything I can use in your defense?"

"Guess not."

"Well, where did you learn to tell fortunes, to read the cards?" Egil asked.

"From an old Romany woman," the old man answered.

"Where? Here in the city?"

"No, it was a long time ago. Bohemia, I think it was."

"Bohemia? You mean Czechoslovakia."

"Yes, that's what they call it now I think. Prague. I was a student there."

"A student? At a university? I thought you didn't believe in learning."

"I was younger then. I thought there were things I might learn. I was wrong."

"Did you get a degree, though? That might carry some weight, especially a foreign one."

"Wait a moment. I think I have one someplace. Let me go look." Schmidts went down to his shop. From below Egil could hear noises as if boxes were being moved around. He didn't quite know what to make of the old man's gypsy tale. Bohemia had become part of Czechoslovakia after the First World War in the breakup of the Austrian Empire. It hadn't been a separate country since the Hapsburgs.

There were footsteps on the stairway and Schmidts showed up with a small picture frame carrying a piece of parchment. It was certainly a degree, but not from the University of Prague. The writing had faded with age and Egil had never learned French, but it appeared to be a doctorate granted by the Sorbonne. It was also made out to one Jacques Krieger.

"This isn't your name."

"It was the name I was using then."

"Can you prove that?"

"Not that I can see."

"Oh well. Maybe we can use it. If you can find anymore old papers like this save them for me. We might have some defense if we can prove you had an education, particularly if it was before the current examination system went into effect."

"I'll do that, Mr. Njalsson."

"Well I've got to get going now. Can I take this with me?" the lawyer asked, holding up the sheepskin.

"Yes, if it will help."

Egil let himself out through the shop. He dumped the diploma on the car seat next to him and started the car. While the engine was warming up he glanced down at it.

The date was written in Roman numerals. It took him a moment to figure out the year. It was 1847. Either the old man was lying to him or he might find himself defending him in a commitment hearing.

The Laws of Magic is available from The Fictional Press. Find it on TheFictionalPress.com, or buy it on Amazon.com now!

The Fictional Detective
By Greg Fowlkes

Now available from
The Fictional Press

Read the first chapter!

THE FICTIONAL DETECTIVE
CHAPTER ONE

I was sitting in my office staring at the frosted glass of the door. It was a cold and rainy Friday morning in October and I had a hangover that made my head feel as faded and peeled as the paint on the walls. The half empty glass of Jack Daniel's wasn't helping my head any, but it was making it easier to ignore some of my other problems. Like how I was going to pay three months back rent on the eight by ten closet the landlord chose to call an office. Jobs had been pretty scarce lately. Even the divorce business had fallen off. No one seemed to care what their spouse was up to anymore. Not for the first time I wondered what the world was coming to.

A sharp rapping sound came that I thought at first was my brain shattering. A second later I realized that it was the tap of knuckles on the glass of the door. The lights were off in the office, and it couldn't have looked very promising from the outside, but the knuckles kept up the rapping. Looking through the "evitceteD ,EDALS KNARF", printed backwards on the frosted glass I could see the form of the rapper silhouetted by the sixty watt bulb in the hallway. It was a woman, and a good looker by the shadow.

The rapping stopped and the shadow moved away. I cursed myself for being too slow, but then she returned and rapped once more. The knuckles had a sort of desperate sound to them so I told her to come in, trying to keep my voice from sounding too harsh. The door opened hesitantly and she stepped through into the darkened office. She stood in the doorway groping for the light switch.

The bank of overhead fluorescents came on with a stutter and the light made me wince. I didn't mind so much when I got a good look at the dame. Her shadow hadn't done her justice at all. She was tall, looking taller on her spiked heels. Her eyes, a soft green gray would have almost been level with my own if I had been standing. Remembering my manners a moment later, I was. She smiled at my courtesy and her warm, red lips almost made my legs melt beneath me. Blonde hair curled under just at her shoulder line. I got a good look at it up close when I stepped forward to help her out of her coat; it looked natural. Everything about her looked natural though she was too good to believe.

I don't normally go overboard treating women with respect. These days it doesn't really pay, but this broad had class. Under her coat she was dressed in a black dress that clung to her like a sheath from her neck to her nylon clad calves, but despite the sensuous curves she looked like she was in mourning.

I held out a chair for her and then took one myself. Self-consciously I put the cap back on the bottle of whiskey and put it and the glass away in a drawer. "What can I do for you, Miss . . . ?" I couldn't see if she had a wedding ring on underneath her gloves, but I had the distinct impression that she wasn't married.

"Janet, Janet Nielsen," she said in a soft voice that reminded me of the taste of good bourbon — smooth and mellow but with a bite to it. "You are Mr. Frank Slade, are you not?"

"That's what it says on the door," I answered. She hadn't made a mistake. I had no illusions about my reputation and Miss Nielsen looked like she had the money and the class to get the best in town.

"I wish to employ your services if you are available, Mr. Slade. It's a matter of some importance to me and I am quite willing to pay you well if you can start immediately."

"I think I can shift my schedule, Miss Nielsen," I said, aware that I had no schedule or clients either. "What is it you want me to do? You didn't correct me when I said 'Miss', so I'm guessing you don't want me to check up on an errant husband. Or do you?"

"No, nothing like that," she said with a note of distaste. "A friend of mine died recently under mysterious circumstances. The police are saying that it was either an accident or suicide. I have reason to believe it was murder."

"Look, Miss Nielsen," I said, "I'd like to help you out, but if its murder, it's a business for the cops and I can't get involved. I could lose my license."

"But if the police say that it's not murder, then you are free to investigate. That's right, isn't it?" she said, assuredly. I wasn't used to getting that much logic out of a woman. "I will pay you two hundred dollars a day plus expenses. That will be adequate, I believe. I have a thousand dollars here as an advance against the first five days."

She opened her purse and pulled out ten crisp, new hundred dollar bills and laid them out on the blotter of my desk. I needed that money, but I was getting a little suspicious of the whole thing. It was too much like the opening of a detective novel; a beautiful woman, a hard boiled private investigator, a stack of brand new large denomination bills.

"Look, I'm still not sure I can do anything for you. Why don't I take a day's pay and check things out with the cops? If I think I can do anything for you, I'll come back and get the rest of the money. If not, we can call it even." I looked into those gray green eyes. She hesitated for a moment, and then nodded. I slid two bills from the pile, and then slid the rest back towards her. She didn't pick them up.

"Okay. Now why don't you tell me who this friend of yours was, and how he died?" I was watching her closely for her reaction as I asked.

"Do you know of Ezekial O. Handler?"

"The mystery writer?" I asked.

"Yes," she answered. For the first time she seemed to lose some of her composure. I wondered why. Handler was pretty well known as a writer. He had written a dozen or more books, a couple of which had made the best seller lists. I'd met him once or twice in the course of my work, but we definitely did not move in the same circles.

"Last night his car went off the road along West Shore Drive. They said it was traveling at a high rate of speed and crashed through the barrier. The car burned and Ezekial burned with it."

"That sounds like an ordinary traffic accident to me, Miss Nielsen," I said, trying not to sound callous.

"But it couldn't have been. He was a very good driver. He never took chances, either. Not stupid ones, at least. He wasn't the kind of man who felt that he had to prove anything, least of all to himself. No, if his car crashed there was a reason for it."

"If there was, I'm sure the police will find it," I said. I didn't like what I had to say next, she obviously had some sort of emotional tie to Handler, but in my business there are a lot of things you have to do that you don't like. "That is if it was an accident. It might have been a suicide. I didn't know Handler personally, but writers aren't always the most stable sort of people. It goes with the artistic temperament. Could he have had any reason for killing himself?"

"No, of course not," she said very defensively. "He had everything to live for. He was well off financially, he had a lot of good friends, he'd just finished his last book and it was one of his best. He stood to make a good deal of money from it, at least a million dollars. He was a happy man, Mr. Slade. I know that he was."

"Just what was your relationship to Handler, Miss Nielsen? Why are you so interested in proving that he was murdered?"

I thought she might clam up then or get huffy, but she said right out loud, "I was his mistress." Just like that, not like she was ashamed of it or anything. Maybe she wasn't. These days who could tell? "I loved him, Mr. Slade, and if he was murdered I want the murderer brought to justice."

I raised my eyebrows at that. Handler had pushed past fifty as far as I knew and he wasn't much of a looker, either. The pictures on his book jackets showed a nose that had been broken in fights a couple of times. When I'd seen him he'd proved to be a short man, though powerfully built. He had a reputation for getting into fights. He didn't seem the sort that would appeal to the woman across the desk from me, but like I always said, who can tell these days.

"I know what you're thinking, that he was thirty years older than me, but I never cared about that. He was always very good to me, kind and gentle. I admit to being a kept woman, Mr. Slade, but that doesn't mean that I didn't love him."

There was something strange about that phrase - kept woman - that seemed out of place. It was more like something from one of Handler's books than what a young, liberated woman should be saying. I didn't doubt that it was true, though. It would explain where Nielsen's money came from. Listening to her, I could believe that she had loved him, too. Either that or she was a mighty good actress.

"I'll take your word for it that he was wealthy and happy, but there are other reasons a man kills himself. What about his past? Could there be some secret there? Or his health? Hemingway killed himself because of cancer, after all." Handler wasn't quite in the same league, but I hoped the comparison might mollify her a little. The last couple of questions hadn't improved her opinion of me.

"I don't know too much about his past. He never talked much about it. He always seemed to live in the present. He's been a public figure for twenty-five years, though. I don't think he could have had many secrets. He never seemed to care what people thought about him anyway, as long as they read his books."

"Maybe he cared about what you thought?" I said.

She smiled at that and I thought I was going to melt again. "No, I don't think so. He was fond of me, but the love was all one way. The only opinions that really matters to him were his own. He never seemed to mind the critics."

"What about his health, then? He was getting on in years."

"I can assure you; he kept in very good shape. He always ran four or five miles before he'd start writing in the morning. He was in good shape other ways, too," she said in a wistful tone that made me wish I'd been the late Mr. Handler. "He'd just been to a doctor a couple of weeks ago for an insurance examination. They must not have found any problems because he got the policy." I could believe her on that. Handler had been something of a physical fitness nut. I could remember the deep chest and the boxer's shoulders.

"Well, we'll rule out suicide for the moment," I said. "But he still might have had an accident. Some drunken fool might have run him off the road. It could have happened. If so, I'm afraid you'll just have to face it. But I'll check with the cops and go out and look at the scene of the crash myself. If I see anything suspicious I'll check up on it, Miss Nielsen."

"Thank you, I'm sure you will. Will that be all, now?"

"Yes, I think so. If I have any more questions I'll get in touch with you." She gave me her address and phone number, then rose to leave.

"Miss Nielsen?"

"Yes?"

"You forgot your eight hundred dollars," I said, though part of me was cursing myself for being a fool.

"Thank you, Mr. Slade," she said, picking up the bills and dropping them into her purse. I helped her on with her coat, smelling again the warm, sweet scent of her hair. Then she was gone.

SCIENCE FICTION AUTHORS RESURRECTED

FYFE RESURRECTED - THE STORIES OF H. B. FYFE

Stories from the Golden Age of Science Fiction by the author of D-99. dealing with the interaction of humans and aliens on far off worlds in ways that were as creative as they were imaginative.

SCHMITZ RESURRECTED - SELECTED STORIES OF JAMES H. SCHMITZ

Includes "An Incident on Route 12", "Watch the Sky", "The Other Likeness", "The Star Hyacinths", "Oneness", "The Winds of Time", "Ham Sandwich" and "Gone Fishing".

SHECKLY RESURRECTED - THE EARLY STORIES OF ROBERT SHECKLEY

Resurrected Press has collected some of the best of these from the 50's including "Warrior Race", "The Leech", "Watchbird", "Warm", "Diplomatic Immunity", "The Hour of Battle", "Besides Still Waters", "Keep Your Shape", "One Man's Poison", 'Ask a Foolish Question", "Cost of Living", "Death Wish Forever".

DICK RESURRECTED - THE EARLY STORIES OF PHILIP K. DICK
Early stories from the author of the novels that inspired "Blade Runner," "Total Recall," and "A Scanner Darkly".

HAMILTON RESURRECTED - CLASSIC STORIES OF EDMOND HAMILTON
Edmond Hamilton was one of the most popular writers during the 30's and 40's, the period that saw the first flowering of modern science fiction.

SMITH RESURRECTED - SELECTED STORIES OF EVELYN E. SMITH
During an era when women rarely appeared in science fiction magazines, Evelyn E. Smith appeared regularly in the pages of Galaxy and Fantastic Universe. Resurrected Press is proud to return these stories to print.

Other Classic Science Fiction Novels
from Resurrected Press

Talents, Incorporated - By Murray Leinster

When a Mekinese fleet conquers his home planet, Captain Bors turns to Talents, Incorporated for help using their collection of individuals with unusual abilities to defeat the enemy and save the galaxy.

The Pirates of Ersatz - by Murray Leinster

Bran Hodden just wanted to be an electronic engineer and marry a delightful girl. But when he's framed by the powers on Walden he's forced to turn back to his family's trade, piracy. Also published as The Pirates of Zan.

Empire - by Clifford Simak

Spencer Chambers and Interplanetary Power owned the Solar System because they controlled the source of power. It fell to Russell Page and Harry Wilson to challenge that control if they had to cross the universe to do it.

Night of the Long Knives - The Creature from the Cleveland Depths - by Fritz Leiber

Two classic novellas set in the not too distant future from a classic master of science fiction.

THE FICTIONAL DETECTIVE
BY GREG FOWLKES

Who killed Ezekial O. Handler?

A beautiful dame, a hard-boiled private eye — and a dead body.

It started like any other case. When a famous writer dies in a mysterious car crash, private detective Frank Slade is called in to find answers, but all he finds is more questions. Who killed Ezekial Handler? Who is Janet Nielsen and why is she so interested in finding out? Who is leaving the neatly typed clues? And as Slade tries to find answers to these questions he starts to wonder if the ultimate answer will threaten his very existence.

Read about it in
THE FICTIONAL DETECTIVE
Visit www.thefictionaldetective.com

The Fictional Press
www.TheFictionalPress.com

About The Fictional Press

The Fictional Press, an imprint of Intrepid Ink, LLC, provides full publishing services to authors of fiction and non-fiction books, eBooks and websites. From editing to formatting, to publishing, to marketing, Intrepid Ink gets your creative works into the hands of the people who want to read them.

Find out more at www.thefictionalpress.com.